Critical Accl

LEFTOVERS

"A riveting story about how far girls will go to protect that which is good and decent in their lives. A bracing, unapologetic, and thoroughly compelling read. I love this book."

—Laura Fitzgerald, author of *Veil of Roses*

SUCH A PRETTY GIRL

"[A] gritty, terrifying novel about a father's abuse of power and trust. . . . Wiess's story is a page-turner that ultimately sends a startling message of empowerment . . . extremely satisfying."

—*Booklist*

"This tale strikes just the right balance between hope and despair, and Meredith's will to survive and ability to take action in the face of her terror are an inspiration."

—*KLIATT*

"This terrifying, powerful novel of child abuse and molestation . . . is perfectly paced, the momentum never slowing as it races toward the inevitable showdown."

—*VOYA*

"In the character of Meredith, Laura Wiess has created a girl to walk alongside Harper Lee's Scout and J. D. Salinger's Phoebe. Read this novel, and you will be changed forever."

—*New York Times* bestselling author Luanne Rice

"*Such a Pretty Girl* is beautifully written and painfully real."

—*New York Times* bestselling author Barbara Delinsky

"Brilliant! *Such a Pretty Girl* hooked me on page one and Laura Wiess's masterful prose kept me turning the pages."

—Ellen Hopkins, author of *Glass* and *Crank*

"*Such a Pretty Girl* is a riveting novel and fifteen-year-old Meredith is a wholly original creation: a funny, wise, vulnerable girl with the heart of a hero and the courage of a warrior. This gut-wrenching story will stay with you long after you finish the last page."

—Lisa Tucker, author of *Once Upon a Day*

"So suspenseful you'll wish you'd taken a speed-reading course. But slow down, because to rush would mean missing Laura Wiess's wonderfully precise language, her remarkable access to Meredith's darkest emotions, and a shocker of an ending, which you'll want to read twice."

—Tara Altebrando, author of *The Pursuit of Happiness*

"In clear, riveting prose, Laura Wiess boldly goes where other writers fear to tread. *Such a Pretty Girl* is gritty yet poetic, gut-churning yet uplifting—a compelling, one-of-a-kind read."

—A. M. Jenkins, author of *Repossessed*

Also by Laura Wiess

Such a Pretty Girl

Available from MTV Books

leftovers

laura wiess

POCKET BOOKS MTV BOOKS

New York London Toronto Sydney

POCKET BOOKS, A Division of Simon & Schuster, Inc.
1230 Avenue of the Americas, New York, NY 10020

This book is a work of fiction. Names, characters, places, and incidents either are products of the author's imagination or are used fictitiously. Any resemblance to actual events or locales or persons, living or dead, is entirely coincidental.

First MTV Books/Pocket Books trade paperback edition January 2008

POCKET and colophon are registered trademarks of Simon & Schuster, Inc.

For information about special discounts for bulk purchases, please contact Simon & Schuster Special Sales at 1-800-456-6798 or business@simonandschuster.com

Manufactured in the United States of America

10 9 8 7 6 5 4 3 2

Library of Congress Cataloging-in-Publication Data

Wiess, Laura
Leftovers / Laura Wiess.—1st MTV books/Pocket books trade paperback ed.
p. cm.
Summary: Two teenagers, Blair and Ardith, lose their innocence in more ways than one as they are transformed from happy ninth-graders to high school sophomores determined to secure justice for their families and friends, whatever the cost.
[1. Family problems—Fiction. 2. Coming of age—Fiction. 3. Friendship—Fiction. 4. Rape—Fiction. 5. Police—Fiction. 6. Self-realization—Fiction.] I. Title.
PZ7.W6372Lef 2008
[Fic]—dc22 2007012836

ISBN-13: 978-1-4165-4662-7
ISBN-10: 1-4165-4662-6

For my mother, Barbara,
and my sister, Sue,
with love.

Acknowledgments

Heartfelt appreciation goes to my agent Barry Goldblatt for his enthusiasm, skill and insight, and to my editor Jennifer Heddle, whose generous guidance and expertise made *Leftovers'* path to publication a real pleasure. You guys are the best.

Sincere thanks to Louise Burke, Jacob Hoye, Erica Feldon, Lisa Keim, Aimee Boyer, Lauren McKenna, and Lisa Litwack at MTV/Pocket Books for their invaluable support and assistance.

Amanda Jenkins, Melissa Wyatt, Mary Pearson, Nancy Werlin, and the YAC list members deserve very special thanks, as do critique group members Shelley Sykes, Lois Szymanski, Livy Sykes, and Terri Coppersmith.

I'm grateful to the Petose and the Wiess families and to Bonnie and John Verrico for their unflagging love, support and encouragement.

But most of all, thanks to my husband, Chet, and my family who, with love, humor and typical Battyanyi determination, have always gone above and beyond to make this girl feel lucky.

We can cure physical diseases with medicine
but the only cure for loneliness, despair, and hopelessness
is love.
There are many in the world who are dying for a piece of bread
but there are many more dying for a little love.

—Mother Teresa

I hold it to be the inalienable right of anybody
to go to hell in his own way.

—Robert Frost

Chapter 1

Blair

Well.

This is harder than I thought it would be.

I wish we could have come over and hung out with you before all this, even once, for like a picnic or something. We would have really liked that. I'm not saying it to make you feel bad, I swear. I'm just saying.

You have a nice yard. It looks lived-in. This is a good patio, too. I like how the bricks are so worn down, like they've been here a really long time.

I know. I have to start, I do, but . . .

Maybe I should sit next to you instead of across from you. It'll probably be easier if we don't have to look at each other. I mean, *I* can look at you, but you shouldn't be turning your head in that neck brace, anyway.

Wait, let me pull this other lounge chair into the shade.

Ouch. There. That's better. I hope your wife won't mind me messing up the seating.

No, I know. She seems really nice. I just said it because . . . I don't know.

You don't have an ashtray anywhere, do you?

Yeah, no kidding, but at this point do you really think it matters? I mean, I'm kind of past getting grounded for smoking.

Okay, I'll use it, but don't blame me if the ashes kill your begonias.

You know, all things considered, you're still pretty good-looking for an old guy.

I'm glad that made you smile. And I'm glad you remember that night. Ardith and I remember everything about every single time we saw you.

It's not baloney. It's the truth. And I'm not crying. I don't do that.

The events leading up to this? Sure, I'll tell you what happened—that's why I'm here—but you're not going to like it, which definitely makes this the hardest thing I'll ever do.

Because when I'm done you're never going to want to see us again.

Ever.

I'm not *assuming* anything. I *know*.

But me and Ardith talked about it on the way here, and we decided that no matter what happens after this, we still want you to know everything. If anybody's entitled to the whole truth, it's you.

Can I have a sip of your ice water, please? Thanks.

In my own words? Okay, then, just remember that you asked for it.

By the time you hit fifteen, there are certain survival lessons you'd better have learned.

Like, that breasts are power. Sad to say, but it all comes down to a matter of supply and demand. Girls have them, guys want them. Even a skank is a hot commodity if she can offer up anything more than a couple of mosquito bites. Not saying she *should* offer them up, just saying she should recognize her advantage and not put out every time some guy manages to string together a couple of compliments.

Too bad that's all it takes sometimes.

Being user-friendly doesn't mean you're going to be loved. Getting attention is not the same thing. Sometimes it's the exact opposite.

And while we're talking about being used and abused, you should know that there are some things you tell and some things you handle by yourself, the best you can. You can't always rat and still hope to be saved when somebody does you wrong. The backlash will dog you till you die.

Or till you wish you were dead.

See, guys freak *out.* They hit critical mass and blast nuclear, white-hot anger out over the world like walking flamethrowers.

But girls freak *in*. They absorb the pain and bitterness and keep right on sponging it up until they drown.

Maybe that's why nobody's real worried about girls going off and wreaking havoc. It's not that the seething hatred and need for revenge isn't there, hell no. It's just that instead of erupting and annihilating our tormentors, we destroy ourselves instead.

Usually.

You root for us in the movies, you know. You want the victims to rise up, sick of being bullied and strike back, winning one for all the little guys who aren't powerful, beautiful, popular, or rich. But when our anger becomes reality, it's a different story.

No, I'm not threatening anyone. It's a little late for that. I'm only pointing out that real life isn't like the movies. The victim doesn't usually win. She just endures.

Prime example: third week of high school there was a sophomore who thought the senior guys she'd started hanging out with were kidding when they herded her into the boys' room so she could supposedly go down on the only one of them who'd never gotten a blow job.

Well, they weren't joking. Word swept the grapevine that she'd done it surrounded by an audience, but she never told the teachers or got any of the guys in trouble.

Why? Because shame shut her up. You could see it in her face, and her walk.

She was known as "that girl who blew the guy in the boys' bathroom" for a few days, but then her screwup was buried under the rubble of the next school scandal and they practically forgot her existence.

So sometimes what takes you down can be used to raise you up again.

But if she'd told instead of handling it privately, it never would have died. Teachers get involved, then parents, cops, and lawyers. The guys' side would stand up and yell, "Well, what did she expect? Why did she go with them? Boys will be boys!"

And then *her* side would insist the boys scared or forced her, and ask why the parents didn't raise their sons better than that, and on, and on.

So no one but her friends really understood why she went with them in the first place.

Because she was a *sophomore*, fresh out of junior high—you know our junior high goes up to ninth grade, right?—and totally bedazzled by the attention. Anyone could see it. These guys walked her to class, bought her lunch, flirted and paid homage to her fine new body. She wanted them to like her so she went along with the joke, not realizing it wasn't a joke until someone was pushing her to her knees, and someone else was guarding the door, and someone else had unzipped his jeans.

She could have hollered for help but if no one came before they shut her up they might have done worse, maybe even hurt her so she wouldn't name them. And besides, if a teacher *did* hear, that would have gotten them all, including her, in deep trouble. Detention. Suspension and notes home. Counselor visits. And how would she explain that on her college application, or to her parents? How would she explain that playing queen to their court jesters had somehow gotten twisted into being led to the bathroom at the deserted end of the hall? How would she explain the stony chill of the tile under her knees when the laughing stopped, and the air grew thick with anticipation?

Stupid, but up until that minute she'd probably believed what they'd told her, that being called a "tease" was worse than actually being a slut, and that nobody liked teases because they never followed through.

I bet she didn't know she could take herself back, that just because a horny group of players called her a tease it didn't mean she was obligated to change their opinion. They were seniors. She was a straight-A, marching band sophomore. You tell me.

What do you mean, how do I know all this? I'm a girl, remember? And no, it wasn't me, but how many of us do you really think make it through without scars?

So by the time you're fifteen you should know all of that, and this, too.

Never bow before your tormentors. Not even if they've locked on to the most humiliating moment in your life. If you don't break, then they have nothing and it's lousy sport and they'll turn their attention to some other poor slob who's wearing a bunched-up maxipad and bleeding through her khakis.

Never let them know you're vulnerable, especially when you are.

Never trust someone else to protect you, and never forget that every choice you make is on you. Ignorance of the outcome doesn't exempt you from the consequences.

This is what you should know by sophomore year, if you want to survive. Too bad we learned the hard way and didn't pass it on in time.

The video camera's running so, for the record, I'm Blair Brost. I'm fifteen.

You'll want to talk to Ardith now.

Chapter 2

Ardith

Are you okay? Do you need a pain pill or anything?

Well, if you do, tell me, and I'll go get your wife.

This is so strange, being here like this. Sitting next to you and all.

I used to think about talking to you a lot. Did Blair tell you we'd dream up fake emergencies to call in, hoping you'd be the one they'd send out?

No? Well, we never actually did it. We were afraid you'd be mad at us for lying.

I guess it's okay to smoke, since the flowerpot's full of Blair's butts.

How long? Umm, I guess about a year. Same as Blair. My parents buy cartons and whoever needs a pack just buys it off them. It's easier that way.

Yeah, I know. Someday half the kids in New Jersey are probably going to hire Blair's mother to sue my parents for giving them cancer, but that's their problem, not mine. As far as I'm concerned, they all deserve each other.

Camera's running? Okay, I guess I'll start.

I know Blair talked a little about sophomore year, but that's really the end of it, and we need to go back to eighth grade, which is when it all began.

"It?" Well, I guess that'd be the first hard lessons bridging the gap between little kid and teenager. Not that we didn't learn plenty beforehand, but there's a difference between being TV jaded and actually being backed against a Burger King wall and groped by a kid with fast hands and sharp braces.

Do you see what I mean? One is fake, like thinking you know all about girls from surfing porn sites, and the other is real, where you choose whether to spit or swallow your blood after his braces slash your lips and discover that the stench of broiled burgers will always be background to your first French kiss.

That's when you start realizing your "firsts" aren't going to be the way you dreamed they would, and that you're feeling lost and stupid, inching your way around a whole new world. Each day brings a different worry like hairy armpits, periods, and BO, and wondering if you really *are* only worth your cup size. You start keeping your opinions to yourself because they might be dumb and you hate yourself for doing it, but it seems safer to blend in than stand out. And yet you *want* to be noticed, but only by being the-same-but-different, and nothing about that confuses you. The reactions to your new body do, though; you strut and show for guys in your school, but shudder when an old man leers, because you don't know how to twitch his crawling gaze off your skin.

So while you're stumbling around trying to get a grip on who you're going to be tomorrow without losing who you were yesterday, suppose your parents decide to throw a bad wild card into the mix.

And I mean a real killer.

I'll go get Blair.

Chapter 3

Blair's Story

When your mother finally makes partner in a prestigious law firm, she decides it's time to buy one of the big, new McMansions across town. She says you need a new house because you've outgrown your current one, a cozy cape in a mostly blue-collar neighborhood, but that's not really true, because besides you and your parents, the only other living thing in the house is your old golden retriever Wendy Darling, and she doesn't take up much space. She's slept in your room for the last fourteen years, first in your bed, but now on her orthopedic mattress next to your bed.

You don't want to move and say so, but nobody cares.

"Appearances count, Blair," your mother says in passing. She's always in passing these days, locked in an unofficial war for Alpha Female with the county's new assistant prosecutor, Jeanne Kozlowski, a soaring legal eagle with unshakable confidence and a stellar conviction rate. They haven't battled each other in court yet, but your mother has been gunning for it since the AP arrived.

Her life is all about winning now, and so even when she glances your way the moment isn't yours, it's only a scenery check. "Judges don't live like this."

"You're not a judge," you say as she gathers her briefcase and an armload of files and heads for the front door.

"Yet," she says and whisks out.

So you target your father, waiting up until he gets home and pestering him until he can no longer avoid a confrontation. You beg not to move and follow him through the house, pointing out all the memories you've made there.

The hallway where, when you were five, you carefully pasted vintage stamps from his collection onto the wall, then enclosed them in a wavy, red crayoned heart. You were proud of your handiwork but he was furious and wouldn't even talk to you for a week.

Halfway through the memory you realize your mistake and rush him on to others.

The thin grooves carved into the kitchen doorway molding, the right side for you, the left for Wendy, one for each year of your lives, showing how tall you'd grown from twenty inches at birth and Wendy from ten inches high as a puppy.

The window at the breakfast bar where, ages ago on an Easter morning while your mother was making cheese omelets and you were filling up on jelly beans, your father lifted the screen, reached out, and snapped a slim, supple branch off the flowering forsythia bush, then gave it to your mother because it was almost as pretty as she was.

He listens to it all, expressionless. "You'll make memories in the new house, too," he says when you pause for breath, and then sends you to bed.

You're not willing to give up, so you change tactics and pitch a fit, but it doesn't matter because nobody's listening. You don't make the money, so you don't have a vote.

Miserable, you sulk, draw a skull and crossbones on the calendar over "moving day," and confide your worries to Wendy, who creaks up off her special mattress, wags her tail, and nuzzles your face. You smooth her silky, blonde hair, gaze into her soft, chocolate eyes, and love her more than anything. She's the sister you never had, and you don't care if she's starting to have accidents in the house, because that's what paper towels are for.

Except on the Thursday before the Monday move your parents show up at your bedroom door together. This sets off an alarm inside you because they're never home at the same time anymore and they never, ever stand in your doorway in a two against one.

"We hope you'll be mature about this, Blair," your mother says, rubbing the end of her eyebrow where the mole used to be. The melanoma was caught in plenty of time and the scar is barely noticeable but she worries it when she's tense; it's a constant, bitter reminder that silent mutinies are the most dangerous.

"It's for the best," your father says, avoiding your gaze.

You slide off the bed and onto Wendy's mattress as the clenched fist in your stomach digs deeper. Sling your arm around her neck, press your cheek to hers, and wait.

"I know how attached you are and I'm sorry it has to be this way, but she'll be happy in her new home," your mother says, and now her words are brisk and purposeful.

"No stairs to climb," your father chimes in with a big, fake smile.

Your mother looks at him and they exchange a quick, silent eyeball message.

Wendy Darling is trembling. Or is it you?

"She's old, Blair, and she's incontinent," your mother says, stepping into the room and stopping at the look you give her. "I found another puddle by the door last night."

Incontinent. The word in adult diaper commercials that means peeing yourself, and worse.

"She's already ruined half the rugs in this house, and we can't allow it in the new one. Not after spending so much money."

"What are you saying?" you ask in a voice helium-high.

Another eyeball message.

Your father the corporate attorney, the interpreter of contracts packaged in Ralph Lauren glasses and a Brooks Brothers suit, says, "We found a home for Wendy, Blair."

"She already *has* a home," you say, because they know how it is with you and Wendy. You're each other's history, she's your other half, and the house you come home to after school is never empty or lonely because she's always there, happy and—

"She can't possibly come with us." Your mother's precision-trimmed hair swings as she shakes her head, then settles flawlessly back into place. "The new house is in showcase condition and it has to stay that way. I won't have her ruining what I've worked so hard to accomplish." Frowning, she picks a dog hair from her navy blue suit jacket and drops it in your wastebasket. "There really is no other choice."

"Because she's incontinent," you repeat, blinking back tears. You know that emotional witnesses lose credibility.

"She's old, hon," your father says, "and whatever time she has left should be peaceful. Put your feelings aside and do what's best for her. She's not going to live forever, you know."

No one is, you jerk, you think, but the thought is swept away on the panic swirling inside your head. You rise, pick up your phone, and dial. You have no words until the call connects and then you know exactly what you're going to say. "Hello, Grandma?" Your voice wobbles. "I'm sorry, but you can't bring Grandpa to our new house because he's incontinent and he'll ruin the rugs, and my mother—"

Your mother snatches the phone from your hand and smoothes things over while your father gives you his "gravely disappointed" look.

You tune them out and hunch down on the mattress next to Wendy. They won't give her away. They can't. She's all you have.

Your mother hangs up. Her mouth is tight and her cheeks red, the way they always are whenever she has to talk to Grandma, only now it's aimed at you. "Well, that was rude. You'll have to call and apologize or I'll never hear the end of it."

You close your eyes and bury your face in Wendy's shoulder.

"Did you hear me, Blair? I just defended you and now I expect a little cooperation in return," your mother says, panty hose swishing as she brushes by, leaving a faint jasmine scent in her wake. "Let's not make Wendy's departure any more unpleasant than it has to be, all right?"

"No." Your voice breaks. "Don't, Mom. I'll take care of her, I swear. I'll take her out every hour, or we could sleep in the kitchen, or I could—"

"This isn't resolving anything," your father says, checking his watch. "Why don't we talk about it again tomorrow?" After a long, pregnant moment, they leave you to yourself.

When you finally stop crying, you brush Wendy's hair until it glows and scratch her favorite itchy spot. You fluff her blanket and take her out three times so she doesn't pee in the house and your parents will see that yes, there *is* another option and you're responsibly pursuing it.

When you get home from school on Friday the air is full of Wendy but the rooms are vacant. At first you think she must be hiding somewhere among the moving boxes, but while you're ripping through the house you notice her squeaky toys are gone. Her orthopedic mattress is gone.

Everything is gone.

You close your eyes, put out your hand, and invisible molecules gather and curve beneath it to form the sleek contours of her head. You know her by heart, you've spent your life learning her by heart, and now your heart is gone.

You jab out your father's office number.

"Where is she?" you say when he answers.

"Calm down," your father says. "Your mother said everything went well and Wendy's resting peacefully in her new—"

"Where?" you demand as a roaring rage fills the pit where your heart used to be.

"It's a very nice place," he says.

"WHERE?" you scream, because he's avoiding a direct question, and you've heard your mother say a thousand times that evasiveness is a red alert. "What did you do with her?"

"Don't shout at me," your father says, shocked. "I'm not telling you where because you're not going to see her and raise false hopes. Your mother and I agreed that if you want a new dog we'll find a reputable breeder and pick out something small, with a pedigree and a return policy in the event of defects. Maybe a Westie or—"

"I don't want another dog!" You slam down the phone. The room shimmers with queer, black speckles and you blink, but they stay. You stagger out to the garbage cans at the road and pry off the lids, throwing them into the street and digging through bags until you find what you were hoping desperately not to see.

The orthopedic mattress.

You pull it out. Smell the sunny, grassy scent. Dig deeper and find the toys, the unused dog food, the blanket, chew bones . . . and her outside lead.

You dump the cans out onto the driveway and sort through the rest, but it's no use. Her leash and collar are gone.

You pile her things inside the fuzzy, plaid blanket and carry it away, leaving the trash strewn across the sidewalk and the empty cans rolling in the road. Dread drives you stumbling to the telephone.

You call Wendy's vet and say, "I'm calling about Wendy Darling Brost. She was brought in t . . . today . . . p . . . p . . . put to sleep there t . . . today . . ." You pause but no one interrupts to say you're wrong and your knees dissolve to gray water.

"Yes?" the voice says politely, urging you on because there are other animals, *live* animals, to care for now. "How can I help you?"

You can't, you can't. "I want her cremated," you say when you're able to speak. "I want her ashes put in an urn."

"Mmm, it's a little late to change disposal plans. Her remains may have already been picked up. Hold, please." She clicks off.

Her remains. Wendy died without you. When? Why didn't you feel it, why didn't your heart skip when hers stopped?

The voice returns. "You're in luck. The pet service is making a run to the crematory and she'll be ready tomorrow. How do you want to pay for this?"

For a minute, all you can think is that Wendy's still there and you should go to her, tell her she's not alone anymore, that you've found her and will bring her back home where she belongs.

But you're fourteen. You have no money and no ride. She weighs eighty-four pounds and she's dead. The vet will never send you home lugging a corpse in a giant Hefty bag.

Your parents knew she was going to die. They *knew*.

"Mrs. Brost?" the voice says impatiently. "How did you want to pay for this?"

Oh. She thinks you're your mother. You decide to let her.

"How much is it?" you ask, hoping it's at least three thousand dollars, the price of one bedroom's new carpeting.

But the figure's low, only two hundred dollars. You tell her to hold on and run to the filing cabinet where your mother keeps the paid credit card bills. Grab one, return, and read her the Visa number. Hold your breath until she says fine.

Good, because now you also want the ashes put in the prettiest container they have and FedExed to your new address. Charge everything.

You request a lock of hair from Wendy's sweeping, feathered tail.

The voice says, yes, of course, I'll include it in the package with her ashes.

You hang up and drag to your feet. Think about calling your father back and screaming, "Liar!" but then he'll know you know, and he might call the vet's and discover what you've done. So you replace the Visa bill, trudge back outside, and clean up the scattered garbage with your bare hands. Right the cans and jam on the lids.

And you learn how completely you can hate.

Alone now and surrounded by silence, you sink deep into your memory, where Wendy romps without arthritis, licks your chin, and solemnly offers you her paw, where you can close your eyes, rest your head on her shoulder, and weep.

You don't talk to your parents when they get home, no, you don't even see them because if there is any fairness in the world, then they will no longer exist.

So you erase them but you don't leave them alone because you want them to see *you*, you want to remind them that they killed your heart and now you will ruin their anticipation. Your ominous silence roils with accusations and you become the big, indigestible lump in their oatmeal, the unanticipated glitch spanning the trade between the McMansion and the murdered dog. You can't let it go and they hate it.

And you feed on that.

You meet the movers at the house on Monday and lug one special carton up the center hall staircase to your cavernous room. FedEx arrives and you intercept the package. Carry it to your room, where you open the carton and lay the orthopedic mattress in the corner near your bed. On it you arrange squeaky toys and the plaid blanket.

From the bottom of the box, you remove the "Rainbow Bridge" poem you printed off an online pet memorial site and the pack of pushpins you're going to use to punch holes in the perfect, unspoiled length of wall. Read the poem, most lines silently, some escaping in a broken whisper.

". . . never to be parted again . . . you look once more into the trusting eyes of your pet . . . then you cross the rainbow bridge together."

You wipe your cheeks and tack the poem on the wall near your headboard. Open the package and lift out an iridescent glass urn lit with the warm, glowing hues of late-afternoon sunlight.

"Blair, what came FedEx—"

You lift your head and watch your mother's gaze bounce from

the urn to the blanket, watch her face register shock, guilt, then settle into her watchful attorney mode. She pulls the bill of lading from the sleeve, skims it, and rubs her eyebrow.

That's when your anger opens wide.

"Murderer," you say.

"Watch your mouth," she says, folding the bill and wedging it in her back pocket. "I know you're upset, but you need to remember who you're talking to." She sighs and tucks her hair behind her ears. Her nail polish is perfect. "All right, Blair. I'm sorry Wendy had to be put down, and I'm sorry you felt obligated to discover it. I was trying to make it easy on you. She lived a long, full life, and I promise she didn't even feel it."

"How would *you* know?" You can't stop seeing her arms locked around Wendy, holding her down as the deadly needle punctures the vein. "You've never been murdered by someone you trusted."

"Oh, haven't I?" she mutters, then flicks a dismissive hand. "Listen to me. I know right now it feels like you'll never get over this, but you will. Sometimes we have to make sacrifices to gain things of greater value. Unfair but true. This is a new beginning for us all and there are some wonderful opportunities waiting to be claimed." Her words are calm and deliberate, a logical, well-rehearsed speech doled out in a tone that implies any further argument means you're either brain dead or asking for trouble.

You feel like kicking her.

"Look around you. Look at this magnificent room. At this *house*." Now her voice swells, alive. "Your father didn't make this happen, Blair. I did. I'm a damn good defense attorney and the youngest person ever to make partner in my firm, not to mention the first woman. All eyes are on me now and there's no room for error. There's already been talk of my being nominated for a position on the bench." She paces and your bedroom becomes a courtroom stage. "I'm willing to do what it takes to make that happen. Win high-profile cases. Cultivate powerful connections. Kozlowski may be the golden child now, but this is the big league and she's playing hardball with the best. Me."

You tilt the urn and something inside it clinks against the glass. A bone? A tooth?

"So from now until I make judge, everything has to be perfect. We need to shine. We couldn't do that in our old house and we certainly couldn't do it with Wendy making a mess everywhere." She shakes her head. "It's a shame, I know. She was a good dog and we'll miss her, but we have to keep moving forward. Do you understand?"

No, and you don't care to. This isn't about *her life;* it's about Wendy's death.

"Blair? I'm talking to you."

The urn is cool beneath your fingers. You wonder how long and hot a fire has to rage to leave nothing but ashes.

"All right, fine. Be angry, if it makes you feel better. My workload has doubled, so you won't be seeing much of me for a while anyway," she says, frowning at the poem tacked to the wall. Tomorrow you know she'll order an assortment of color-coordinated picture frames. "Your father's going to try to get home from his office a little earlier to compensate, but you know the kind of behavior we expect and you're old enough to handle your time wisely. The interior decorators will be in this week and I've hired a housekeeper who'll come during the day. I'll show you how to set the alarm so you'll feel safe after dark—"

"So you planned to kill her a long time ago," you say, placing the urn on the nightstand so your grip doesn't shatter it. "That makes it premeditated." Her leaden silence affords you a moment of mean pleasure.

"I don't know why I even bother to try," your mother says finally, rubbing her forehead. "Go ahead, play the victim. Ignore all the wonderful things this new life has to offer and cling to the one sacrifice you had to make to get here. But I'm telling you now, Blair, you're not going to ruin it for the rest of us." She looks away, waiting.

You wait, too, clinging to the memory of your sacrifice and letting the silence speak for you. There is nothing she can say that will ever alter what she and your father have deliberately done. You've spent years listening to her discuss the various levels of intent and you know how damning it can be. A screwdriver is an inanimate object, until wielded by a hand with violent intent and stabbed into someone's eye. A syringe full of poison will lay on an examining table forever, harmless until someone wants to kill a dog.

The stalemate stands. She leaves.

You close your door after her. Lock it.

And dwell on intent.

Thank you. I'm sorry about Wendy, too.

I'm glad you didn't say, "Be reasonable, Blair. She was just a dog." I would have hated to start hating you.

Yeah, I know I've changed. Nothing gets to me anymore.

Well, okay, except for the stuff in the past. Back then I was all innocent and trusting and didn't know anything. Now I know plenty and you can't fucking touch me.

Oh God, I'm sorry. That didn't come out right. But I guess nothing really ever does, does it?

After my parents killed Wendy and we moved into the mausoleum—which is exactly what that stupid house was, seeing as how I was usually the only one ever in it—eighth grade let out and I kind of got lost. The interior decorators did their thing. Lourdes, the housekeeper, came, cleaned, and left dinner in the fridge. Her son Horace planted all these tortured, twisted bushes and weeping midget trees. He drank from the hose, ate his lunch on the tailgate of his pickup, and made sure he was gone before the parade of Mercedes hit the cul-de-sac at dusk, beelining up their driveways and straight into their garages.

The landscapers were the only ones in the development that I ever saw get dirty.

Horace? No, I didn't really talk to him. I was too depressed to talk to anybody. Not even Ardith, who kept trying to open me up somehow. And when I think about what she was dealing with at the time, well, I give her a lot of credit for sticking by me.

I mean, you know about Ardith's family.

No, in the beginning I didn't really know how bad they were. Well, I guess I *knew,* but I didn't really believe what she told me. It's not that I thought she was lying; it's just that my life was so different that I couldn't understand hers without actually experiencing it.

But that's for later, along with the whole miserable Dellasandra mess.

For now I'll just say there's always one hangout house in town where the parents are "cool" and almost anything goes.

Ardith's was it, and she hated it.

Chapter 4

Ardith's Story

Unlike Blair, who's an only child, you're the baby of the family. You have a seventeen-year-old brother and an older sister. That makes your parents up there in age, since your sister's twenty-five and you're fourteen, but you seem to be the only one who realizes it.

Your mom dyes her hair Goth black, wears eyelet-trimmed Daisy Dukes, halters, and shiny, lip-plumper gloss. She laughs too loud and overlooks too much, especially when she's drinking. She sits by the pool in a crocheted bikini, flirts with your brother's friends, and says she's only thirty-five, but the rose tattoo on her breast is becoming long-stemmed and sort of crinkly. She's embarrassing.

Your father's a faded lion, a slack-muscled, shaggy-haired ex-utility worker out on permanent disability for a work-related foot injury. He tells his glory days stories over and over again, roaring his rockabilly talent show triumph, purring about all the girls he had before getting your mom pregnant in college. Given the beer and the time, he'll ramble on about the Cuban cigars he handed out for your brother's birth, his thirty-year high school reunion singing comeback, and the lucky break that brought him early retirement, ending the saga with a wet grin and a good-natured, "I stepped in dog shit, fell on my ass, and *still* came out smelling like a rose." He sells used adult movies at the flea market for extra cash, shaves his monobrow, and has an endless repertoire of twangy songs that makes him sound like he's from anywhere but New Jersey. He sings the first verse of "Lawdy Miss Clawdy" when he joins your brother's friends on the deck for a few beers, sucking in his belly and wearing baggy shorts that gap when he sits, proving he doesn't wear underwear. He cops feels off your brother's girlfriends and his favorite ambush site is the bathroom hallway.

"Uh-oh, dirty old man on the loose," he'll croon, flexing his fingers and backing his chosen one up against the wall. "You have to pay a toll to get through."

And his victim will laugh, nervous and grossed-out by his stale breath and hooded gaze, but she doesn't want to piss off your father, who has the power to ban her from the house, so she'll play along and try to slip by unscathed. But your father is good at what he does. Few escape his touch.

The girls endure it because your brother's a hot bad boy with bedroom eyes, a killer smile, and a dangerous edge, and the house is a haven where partying is the norm and no one proofs you when you kick in for beer. There's always a place to crash, even if you do wake up sometimes with an anonymous hand trying to slip between your legs.

So you learn to padlock your door both coming and going and turn a deaf ear to the jeers as you tackle your homework. You call your parents Connie and Gil, because they hate the heavy tags of

Mom and Dad, and buy baggy, boring clothes so your mother won't borrow them. Your hair is short because the guys like it long and your bras are minimizers, designed to flatten the C cup you inherited from your mother.

You keep your dream of becoming a podiatrist to yourself because the one time you mentioned it, your mother said, "Why?" and your father smirked and said, "I should have been a gynecologist," and your brother laughed and said, "Great, a freak with a foot fetish." Your older sister is a financial advisor and never comes home to visit. You wish *you* could never come home to visit, too, but the only place to go is Blair's and she's been too distracted by moving and some kind of private misery to offer you sanctuary.

So when the public pool opens in June and the swim dance is announced, you latch on to it because it will keep you away from your own pool, where the drinks flow and skinny-dipping after sunset is the norm, not the exception.

You wear your bathing suit under your clothes and meet Blair down at the park at 8:30. You cut across the football field toward the fenced area and the faint, laughing shrieks from this pool are nothing like the forced-humor cries of "Gil, stop it!" from the high school girls when your father sinks beneath the surface to play pinching crab.

You wonder why your brother lets your father do it, and why your mother acts like she doesn't know. And you remember snatches of conversation between the girls, warning each other to steer clear of the lech, and wonder what they would say if you told them that everytime he gets drunk, you're not sure being his daughter will continue to grant you immunity.

You and Blair drop your towels under a tree and strip. Her bathing suit is last year's and her breasts are too big for the top. Before you think, you poke the pale side of one soft overflow and say, "Hey, who do you think you are, Pamela Anderson?"

Her head snaps up and she stares at you, shocked by the trespass, but no more than you are. She snorts, says, "Yeah, right," and you're off the hook, except that your heart is pounding and you're almost tempted to reach out and do it again.

You don't, though, because through major effort you've managed to separate your home experiences from your public life, and it scares you that the lines just blurred.

"Hey," Blair says, grinning. "You cold?"

You glance down at yourself and blush. The sage green, adjustable-strap, underwire bikini top is perfect in all ways but one; it's isn't lined. You didn't even notice it when you bought the suit back in April because the store was overheated and you were so happy to find something underwire that wasn't ugly, but now—

Gary, the ninth grader who kissed you and cut your lip, slouches by in a jostling knot of boys and calls, "Hey Ardith, nice tits!"

Mortified, you cross your arms over your chest, but the damage is done; you can still hear those same words whispered in the dark, prepadlock days at home, right before you woke up flailing and broke your brother's friend's nose.

"He's such a waste," Blair says with a derisive sniff. "C'mon, let's go swimming."

"Okay," you say and keeping your arms folded, pad to the water's edge. Dip a toe.

Blair bullets past and dives, going deep and popping up in the center of the pool. She waves and sloshes toward you. Her dark hair is slicked back and her eyebrows need plucking. "You going to swim, or just stand around showing off?" she says, then grabs your arm and pulls you down into the water.

You play like kids, sinking to the bottom to walk on your hands, racing, diving, gasping, and splashing inside your own shiny bubble. When you stagger out, exhausted, you share a Coke and endure more Gary remarks until Blair finally masters a perfect, drawling, "Like I really give a shit," which she shortens to *lirgas.* The tone, coupled with her attitude, stance, and jutting breasts are too much for him. He gives her the finger and leaves with her hurried "In your dreams" ringing in his ears.

You stay until the end, swimming and playing while the older kids hook up and dance to a local garage band, but when you're cutting back across the parking lot toward the football field, wearing your towel sarong and carrying your clothes, someone calls your name. It's the guy whose nose you broke last year. He's hanging out of an Isuzu, buzzed, and says, "Wanna party?" You look at Blair. She says, "Yes," but you say, "No," because you know the price he'll charge and it's way too high.

So he laughs and rummages around. Yells, "Here, catch!" and you miss it, but Blair doesn't. The Isuzu peels away, leaving her holding a screw-top bottle of fizzy, pink wine.

And something changes.

You walk to the far side of the field and end up under the trees. By mutual, unspoken consent, neither of you are ready to go home yet.

Blair gives you the bottle and her clothes. She spreads her towel on the grass, sits, and holds up her arms for her stuff. You hand it over and spread your towel beside hers. The night is cool, so you hug your knees.

You hear the metallic crackle as Blair fumbles with the cap and watch her pale throat arch as she tilts the bottle and drinks.

"Ack," she says, scowling and rubbing her nose. "Sour bubbles. You should have warned me."

"It wouldn't have stopped you," you say, accepting the bottle.

"Well, no," she says. "But then at least you could have said, 'I told you so.' "

You pass the wine back and forth until it's empty and there's a dark sort of determination about the way you're drinking.

Blair sets the bottle aside and swivels to face you. "I have to tell you something." Her expression is smudgy with shadows and you can hear her breathing.

"What?" you say, going still.

"Wendy was murdered," she says thickly and the story spills out. By the time it's done you're both crying, Blair as though she'll never stop. "It h . . . hurts so m . . . *much*," she whispers and sounds so heartbroken that you cry harder, too, adopting her loss as your own, hugging her and patting her back until her sobs are replaced by staggered, hitching breaths and she eases out of your arms.

You watch as she wipes her face. Tears glisten in her lashes and her bottom lip still trembles. The sight fills you with a rush of love and protectiveness so fierce that it hurts. "Don't be sad anymore, okay?" you say, and in a move you never would have made if you were sober, reach out and touch her cheek. "You still have me."

"I know," she says in a pitiful voice, catching your hand. "You're my best friend now, Ardith. For always, right?"

You nod, throat too tight to speak.

"Good," she says, sniffling and reaching past you for the wine bottle. She tilts her head back and upends it over her mouth, catching the last few drops. "All gone," she says mournfully, dropping it and shivering. "Everything's gone. *Brrr.*" She rubs her bare arms. "Now I'm cold."

"Here," you say, tugging your towel out from beneath you. "We'll share." You move onto her towel and huddle together under yours for warmth. You don't talk about the prickly razor stubble on her leg or the drift of thick, soft hair brushing your shoulder. Instead, lulled by the wine and the glory of your newfound closeness, your reins go slack and you confess what you saw last night when the pool lights were dimmed and everyone thought you were inside, asleep.

You got up to pee. Unlocked your door and went into the bathroom without turning on the light, because lights have a way of drawing pests. When the murmurs penetrated your brain, you stood up without flushing and parted the blinds. In the pool, with the half light casting mermaid spangles across the water, you saw your brother and his current girlfriend bobbing together in the deep end.

You closed the blinds and backed out of the room. Padlocked your door and crept into bed. Thought about all the summer nights ahead and wondered if you can get pregnant from swimming in sperm water. There's no one you can ask.

" 'Sperm water?' " Blair says and catches her breath. "Wait, you mean they were doing it in the pool? Where anyone could see them? No way!"

You nod. "Yes way."

"That's-so-gross," she says, slurring the sentence into one long, run-on word. "I'd never even be able to *kiss* somebody if I knew people could see me."

"Me, either," you say solemnly.

"You guys have a lot of parties," Blair says after a moment. "How come you hardly ever talk about them?"

You lower your head and study your feet. They're sleek, slim, and perfectly arched, elegant even, not that anyone but you has ever noticed. "They're not real parties, they're just my brother's friends, drinking and hanging out."

"Cool," she says wistfully.

You snort. "Sure, if you're a guy. If you're a girl, it can get pretty hairy."

"You know what I mean," she says, bumping you. "God, they're all there, all the time. Don't you want any of them?"

You think of the regulars. Some are cute and some are funny . . . well, before they grope, puke, and pass out. "Nope."

"But they're older guys, and all different ones, like a smorgasbord." She giggles and snakes an arm out from under the towel. "Let's see, I'll have one of those and one of those and oh, let me have a little of that one, too."

You shake your head.

"What?" she says, pouting. "I'm not talking about sex, I'm just talking about . . . I don't know. Love. Romance. Boyfriends. Hanging out. Doing stuff."

"Well, they'll hang out and do stuff to you, all right," you say grimly.

"Oh, stop," she says, laughing. "They wouldn't be like that. I mean, it's not like I'm irresistible or anything." She cocks her head. "Am I?"

"You don't have to be irresistible at my house," you say, because she's missing the point. "You just have to be a girl."

"Well, then, what if I don't drink?" she says, determined to discover the key to the kingdom and finagle some fun out of your household. "Wouldn't that give me the upper hand?"

"A *padlock* gives you the upper hand," you say, running your fingers through your damp hair. "That, or a set of *cojones*."

She sways, burbling with laughter.

"You think I'm kidding," you say, releasing a reluctant grin.

"No, but nothing ever happens at my house. It sucks." She rests her head on your shoulder. "Have you ever seen anybody doing it in real life? I mean, like, out of the pool?"

"Yeah." Drunk people are not shy. "It ain't pretty."

"It is in the movies. But it would be weird to be naked with a guy. I don't even think I'd want to see it, you know?" Silence. "What does it look like?"

"What?"

"*It.* You know." She elbows you. "His thing."

"I don't know," you say, because you don't like knowing so much more than she does.

"You lie," she says, laughing and tickling your ribs. "Come on, Ardith, tell me. Or take me home with you so I can go see for myself."

"Right, okay, stop," you say, because her fingers are making your skin ripple and you would rather burn down your house than bring Blair over there to be mauled by the masses. "It looks like a big red mushroom, okay?"

Her hands still. "Really? They all look like mushrooms?"

"I haven't seen them *all*," you snap.

"No, I didn't mean . . . you know what I mean," she says, poking you. "Don't be mad, Ardith. I just wanted to know."

"I know," you say. "I'm not mad."

"Gary kissed you, didn't he?" Blair asks and you feel the weight of her gaze but there's little to see, because here beneath the pines, the darkness is deepest.

"Yeah," you say.

"I haven't even been kissed yet. I always thought I would be first." She tilts back her head, reels, and clutches your knee. "Whoa, I'm spinning." She laughs and leans closer. "Have you ever been felt up?"

"Does being groped behind a Burger King count?" You mean it as a joke but it comes out breathless; the wine and her heat are making you dizzy. You don't understand it, but you're just blurry enough to indulge it.

"I guess," she says. "What does it feel like? I mean, I've done it to myself but it can't be the same. What are you supposed to do while it's happening?"

"I don't know," you say. "I only got it on the outside and I didn't do anything except push his hand away." And now you're wondering what a soft touch on bare skin would feel like, too. "But don't tell anybody, Blair. They'll think I'm a slut." And you won't be, ever, because you're going to be a podiatrist instead.

"I'll never tell," she promises, dragging her finger across her chest in a little-kid cross my heart. "I wonder what it feels like." She looks at you. "We should find out."

You're not sure what she means. "How?"

She leans close. "Here. Now. Don't you want to know, so that when it happens for real you won't be caught by surprise?"

The pit of your stomach throbs. "I guess." What's "for real"? Are you allowed to disqualify casual pinches, gropes, and whoever corners you next until you choose someone to make it "for real"?

"Good," she says. "So you're the one with the experience. How do we do it?"

"I don't know." You can't look at her. "If we do, does it make us gay?"

"No," Blair says, but she sounds unsure. "I mean, isn't this like playing doctor?"

That hits your funny bone, and your giggles spark her giggles, and before you can catch your breath you're kissing, tasting sweet wine and strawberry lip gloss. Your hand slips up to touch her breast. She stiffens, tentatively touches yours, and somehow both your hands wiggle their way inside of both your damp tops. Breathing blends with cricket chirps and the persistent pounding of blood coursing through your veins.

"Air," Blair gasps, finally pulling away, and that sets you giggling all over again. So does the sight of her hand trapped in your top and yours in hers, so you both tug free and make sure to keep on laughing because you're not quite buzzed enough to excuse what just happened, but the awkwardness must be banished if you're ever to look at each other again.

"So that was it," Blair says and hiccups.

"Yeah," you say as she holds her breath. You turn away, thoughts jumbled, body tingling, bewildered by warring feelings and how easily Blair seems to have recovered. It's embarrassing, this heightened sensitivity, it makes you feel like you got way too into it and it shows. You shake out your T-shirt and slip it over your head. Your coordination is off and you spend a moment battling blindly for the armholes. "Don't ever tell, okay?"

"I won't," she says without breathing. "You, either."

You pop your head through the hole, too unsettled to answer, and are snaking your arms through the sleeves when someone drawls, "Hey, check this out."

Startled, you brush the hair from your eyes and peer up into the darkness at the figures looming over you. It's Gary, the BK Romeo, and his slouchy friends.

"This some kind of lezziefest?" Gary says and grins as his buddies snicker.

Blair shoots you an alarmed look.

You rub your palms together, thinking, smearing away the guilt and searching for a believable comeback. If Gary smells fear, you'll be ruined.

"I could say the same thing about you guys," you say, grabbing the empty wine bottle and rising. "*We* were partying. What're you doing out here alone, playing pocket pool?"

"Kiss my ass," he says, shifting and putting some space between him and his friends. "We were just hanging out on the bleachers. So what. Big deal."

"Oh yeah? Then what're you getting so nervous about?" You keep pushing, mostly because it seems to be working as a diversion. "Afraid we saw *you* doing something?"

"Asshole," he says, turning to leave.

"Takes one to know one," Blair calls after him, scrambling up.

You watch until they're swallowed by darkness, then grab your stuff and run up into the wooded berm, feet pounding, branches slapping and tearing at your hair, but you keep on running until you burst out the other side onto the lane where you bend and breathe, jam your bruised feet into your sneakers, and gasp, "Do you really think they saw anything?"

Laughing, you collapse against each other and are celebrating your escape when the patrol car pulls up. No lights, no siren. You draw apart and realize you're still carrying the empty wine bottle, your shirt is on backward, you lost your towel, and you're wearing one of Blair's sneakers.

A cop steps out of the car. Talks into his radio and starts toward you.

You whisk the bottle behind you and glance at the woods, gauging the distance. Will you make it? You try to signal Blair to get ready to run, but she's too busy pulling twigs from her hair and tugging at her bathing suit to realize what's going to happen.

"Evening, ladies." The cop is tanned and lean, with gray threading his dark brown hair and mustache. He hitches up his gun belt and stops a yard away, calm but ready for you. He smells cool and rich, like winter leather. "Everything okay?"

You're sweating, trying not to squirm as you wedge the empty bottle into the back of your suit bottoms. If Gary bursts out of the woods and sees the bottle in your pants you'll never live it down, but it's still better than getting busted for drinking. Maybe.

"Fine," Blair chirps, beaming at him. "How are you?"

"I'm fine, thanks," he replies. "Where are you girls coming from?"

"The swim dance, can't you tell?" Blair says, holding up a fistful of tangled hair and rolling her eyes. She sways slightly. "Well, not straight from there. I mean, we were there until it ended, but then we were hanging out on the football field and—"

You explode into a tubercular coughing fit. How can a lawyer's daughter be so willing to confess? The bottle slips. You clap a hand to your butt and shift your hip, aiming for attitude while you wedge the bottle down farther. "Shut up, Blair," you mutter, mostly without moving your lips. "He's *not* on our side."

Blair laughs. "Why, because of that?" She points to the bottle. "So what? It's empty. We could have found it in the woods or something."

"But you didn't," the cop says. "Let's have it." He holds out his hand.

You should run, with or without Blair. Save yourself. But you won't.

"Well?" he says, pinning you with his gaze.

Defeated, you remove the bottle. Wipe the butt sweat off on Blair's towel, ignoring her indignant look, and hand it over to the cop. Stare at your mismatched sneakers.

"We didn't buy it," Blair says, crouching and rooting through her stuff. She tugs her T-shirt from the pile and wrestles it over her head. Rises and clutches your arm for balance as she struggles into her shorts, and then hands you yours. "Some guy gave it to us."

"So you drank it," he says, sighing. "Come on, ladies, you know better than that. Didn't anyone ever tell you not to take alcohol from strangers?"

"No," Blair says earnestly. "Just candy."

You glance at her, then him, waiting for the ax to fall. His mustache twitches and his silver badge gleams in the streetlight's dull glow. Number 23. His nametag says FINDERNE. He's paying very close attention to you both and doesn't seem easy to fool.

"Are you gonna arrest us?" you ask flatly while you finish dressing.

"Do you have anything else on you that I should know about?" he says. "Drugs, needles, knives . . . ?"

"No," you say, oddly hurt. Does he really think you're that bad?

"We only had that one bottle, I swear," Blair says, twisting the front of her T-shirt into a knot. Her eyes are huge, her face stricken, like she's finally realized what's happening. "Please don't arrest us. Please? We'll get in deep trouble. We didn't m . . . mean to m . . . mess up. My d . . . dog just d . . . died."

"Oh," he says gravely, as if she makes perfect sense. "I'm sorry to hear that."

Blair's eyes puddle with tears. "Me, too. I really loved her."

He pats her shoulder. His hand is square and steady.

A sudden, crippling pang pierces your chest. "I had a dog once," you blurt, flushing as they look at you. "But he got hit by a car because my parents kept leaving the gate open. It was a long time ago. Never mind." You feel like a fool.

"Well, I'm sorry to hear that, too," he says, pulling a pad and pen from his shirt pocket. "Now, what're your names?" His feet are planted flat on the road like he knows you're not going anywhere.

Your words surge again without censor, eager to beat Blair's.

His eyebrows quirk at your last name. "Your brother drives a red Nissan Z?"

You nod, mortified, heat churning your insides. He knows. You should have known he would, since your brother's been picked up for speeding, resisting, and DUIs before. Small comfort that the sex stuff, even the girl who claimed he'd taken her into the woods behind your house and forced her to mess around, has never been reported. God only knows what this cop would think of that.

"Yeah, we've met," Officer Finderne says dryly. "Is he staying out of trouble?"

"I guess," you say, staring at the ground.

"Good," he says. "Why haven't I seen you before?"

"I don't know." Your voice is small. "I spend a lot of time in my room." You swallow hard and force yourself to meet his gaze. "If you arrest me, will you at least let Blair go?" It's a lot to ask, but you think maybe he will because he seems fair and decent, and hasn't said anything gross or ogled your chest even once since he stopped you.

He holds up a hand as if to say "wait" and speaks into the mike hooked to his shirt. After getting a scratchy "10-4" back, he looks straight at you. "Relax, Ardith. You're not your brother and I'm not arresting anyone. Get dressed, and I'll take you both home."

"Really?" You can hardly believe it. "Are you sure?"

He nods, takes Blair's name, and once you finish switching sneakers loads you into the back of the air-conditioned patrol car. "Do your parents know where you are?"

"Nope," Blair says, shivering at the drop in temperature.

"They don't care," you add.

"I'm sure they do," he says, meeting your gaze in the rearview mirror.

You shrug, because you know otherwise.

"Brrr," Blair says, holding herself.

He closes the air vents. "How's that?"

"Better, thanks," she says, smiling.

You scowl and finish unraveling the hem of your T-shirt.

Blair perks up again and says, "You know, you're pretty good-looking for an old guy," earning a startled snort of laughter. She preens and says, "Can't we ride around with you for a while? We'll be good. You won't even know we're here. And if anybody asks, you could tell them we're rookies, training to go undercover. That'd be cool." She catches your frown and frowns back. "Or you could just say we're your kids."

Officer Finderne laughs and shakes his head. "Oh yeah, I'm getting old."

You stop at Blair's house first where, much to her relief, no one is home yet. She lingers on the porch and then goes dutifully inside without incident.

When Officer Finderne—Dave—asks where you live, you steer him to the south side of town. Your house is the last of three on a dead-end street marked "No Outlet," a 1950s ranch stretched indolently across a rumpled, wooded lot.

You weave through the cars clogging the driveway, leading him to the front door. He knocks but no one answers and it's locked, so you motion him around to the back gate in the privacy fence. The two of you walk in on the same scene you've avoided a hundred times, except this time you're not alone, and this time you're feeling righteous.

He takes one look and radios for backup.

Someone yells, "Cops!" and the stampede is on. Officer Dave barks out orders, instructing everyone to line up, empty their pockets, and show ID.

Three of the girls and four of the guys, including your brother, are buzzed and underage. You sit on the steps and watch as your father slips away before backup arrives. Your mother is given a summons for providing alcohol to minors.

You yawn, suddenly sleepy from all that swimming, say good night to your cop, and head into the house.

You pee for what seems like forever, pad into your bedroom, and lock the door, listening to your brother stalk the hall and curse you for being a stupid bitch who doesn't have the sense to drink at home. He body slams the door and you slip the screwdriver out from under your pillow, just in case.

You sneak away early the next morning, stepping over your brother slumped sleeping outside your door and weaving through the overage rejects sacked out in your TV room.

Blair's parents are working, so you spend the day roaming the town, looking for Officer Dave. You buy a big box of Dunkin Donuts to give him as a thank-you but end up eating them yourselves because he must be off-duty and with his own family.

When you finally go home again, your mother grounds you. Your father has taken the padlocks off your door and your brother calls you a mutant and asks how the hell you got into this family anyway. No one swims nude that night—no one swims at all. They just sit around drinking and looking resentful until your mother pulls out the cards and starts a game of poker.

You are not invited to ante up.

So that was the night me and Blair got drunk at the pool. It's important because it changed things, brought us together somehow. I don't know. I mean, we were friends before that, but nowhere near as close as we got afterward.

Plus, we met you.

Wait. Give me a minute, okay? This stirs up a lot of stuff for me.

No, I'm all right. I just need some of that water. Thanks.

Am I sorry about what happened? What're you, kidding?

Oh, you mean about Dellasandra. Yeah. She didn't deserve what she got. You probably won't believe me, but if there had been any other way . . .

You should talk to Blair now. You need to know more, before you can understand how and why this had to happen. But don't push too hard, okay? This last week has been really rough on her. She's lost a lot already, and I don't think she understands that by the time this is over we're both probably going to lose everything.

Well, yeah, a lot of that depends on you.

Me? I didn't have much to begin with. You know that.

Sure, I wanted things. I wanted to be a podiatrist, and I wanted to live where my last name didn't automatically mean loser. Not a lot of places left though, huh? Oh well, what're you gonna do.

You know, Blair tries hard to be tough, but if she really didn't care about what happened, then we wouldn't even be here right now. This whole confession thing was her idea. I hope you'll keep that in mind.

What? Oh. Well, my parents laid low for a week and then everything went right back to normal. The worst times were the mornings, when my father was at the flea market and my mother had her web design classes. I didn't like being in the house with all the hungover guys from the night before, so I put new padlocks on my door and decided climbing out my side window would be a lot easier than running the gauntlet every time I wanted to leave.

Blair had the exact opposite problem.

Chapter 5

Blair's Story

Your parents are so wrapped up in work that you spend most evenings as the mausoleum's sole occupant. Your neighbors are anonymous commuters gone from dawn to dusk, then comfortably burrowed into their air-conditioned castles. Nothing, not even being escorted home from the swim dance by the long arm of the law, seems to net you a moment's notice.

You stand on your doorstep under the porch light, an orphan without a basket, waving good-bye to Officer Finderne and Ardith, then go inside the empty house, lock up, and set the alarm.

But it's not enough.

Something important is missing, and its elusive lure nips at your heels, driving you to find it. You search, circle and pace, frustrated, and finally give up, not sure that you ever actually had what you think you lost anyway.

You've found other things, though, like a file of recent Victoria's Secret shipping confirmations to Amber, hidden in your father's desk drawer. A birthday card to him from her, with a lipstick-print kiss above her signature and a string of XO's, too.

And a legal agreement dated two months ago between your parents, stating your mother will grant your father an uncontested divorce and surrender all assets with the exception of the house, her personal possessions, and financial accounts providing he . . .

The paragraph blurs.

You rub your forehead. Struggle to translate the lawyerspeak.

. . . providing he maintain, uphold, and support his position in the family, conduct his private affairs with discretion, and cause no disruption or scandal until such time as your mother is appointed a judge, or two years from the date of said agreement.

Oh.

There's more, but you can't read it. The print is too small and the words too big to wrestle with after wine. And besides, what else do you need to know?

You replace the document. Stand in the center of their king-size bed and survey both sides of the room. His desk, her desk. His phone, her phone. The same with bureaus, closets, and bathrooms.

The bed is the only common ground.

You put on your mother's perfume and her red silk chemise and wander around the vast, silent tomb. Stand in the bedroom window overlooking the deserted street, waiting to be acknowledged.

A sleek, well-fed Siamese cat sits in the middle of the cul-de-sac. You wave. It jerks its tail and strolls away.

You think about calling your grandmother to say hi but it's late, you're naked under the chemise and it'll be too weird. You think about Ardith's hand in your top and Officer Finderne patting your back, and wonder what would happen if he pulled up to your house right now. Would he stay and talk to you? You don't know, but either way he would probably make you put on your bathrobe.

You leave the window. Tear off the chemise and throw it in the corner.

You remember the night your mother first found out about Amber, how the bulleting words ricocheted off the walls and shot out through the open windows into the old neighborhood. You remember lying on the floor of your room, your cheek pressed into the rug and your ear to the door crack.

"Her name is *Amber*? Are you serious?" your mother said, incredulous. "Oh please, say no more. Let me guess. She's a dancer at the club, a brave, sweet single mom who's only stripping to support her baby, right? No? Okay then, let's go for the *full* clichéd midlife crisis; she's a curvy little twenty-year-old legal assistant who runs for your coffee and gets all pink and breathy every time she sees you, and in her big, worshiping eyes you can do no wrong, and her adoration makes you feel so *young* again. How's *that*?"

"It's impossible to talk to you when you get this emotional," your father said.

You hold your breath, straining to hear what comes next.

"All right then, without emotion; end it, or talk to my lawyer," your mother said.

"Fine, I'll end it," he said.

But apparently he didn't, and apparently your mother doesn't really care anymore, as long as he's discreet and remembers that appearances count.

You root through your bureau and pull on your old *Beauty and the Beast* bathrobe. The terry cloth is worn through in spots, the shoulders are tight and the hem barely brushes your knees, but sometimes you still need to wear it.

You go back downstairs.

The house, decorated by strangers, is elegant and pristine. The family room has a hearth Wendy would have loved.

The pit in your chest blackens, knowing that she died too soon, and for nothing.

Vacation stretches on, hot, hazy, and unremarkable. You sleep late, lie in the sun, wander around online, and do a half-assed job of learning Spanish from Lourdes.

It's the first summer you've ever spent without Wendy.

Your parents come and go, leaving used coffee cups in the dishwasher and the lingering scent of jasmine shower gel in the air, but you rarely see them. When you do, they're on the phone or by the fax machine, checking e-mail or hurrying out the door.

You make no demands or complaints, just watch from the sidelines and your passive exterior seems to reassure them, as they leave you an occasional fifty-dollar bill with an order to *Buy yourself something nice!* Once your father leaves you a note asking if you're ready for that new puppy yet.

You tear it up and flush it down the toilet.

Your mother's archenemy, Jeanne Kozlowski, scores another coup, prosecuting and convicting the township's code enforcement officer on bribery charges. Your mother is rabid over the positive media coverage and your parents become campaign groupies for the party in power, attending political fund-raisers throughout the state. The first time they leave you alone overnight, you and Ardith go on a grocery store spree, buying so much that you have to borrow the shopping cart to get it all home. You scan the streets, wondering if maybe Officer Dave will cruise up and scold you for the stolen cart, but he doesn't.

You carry the bags into the house and Ardith pushes the cart back down to the corner. When she returns, you prepare a feast of garlic bread, spring rolls, and mozzarella sticks. You eat in the family room and for a while the house rings with life and laughter.

Ardith opens a pack of cigarettes and you learn to blow smoke rings while you tap your ashes into a Waterford crystal vase and wonder aloud who your first real boyfriends will be, shrieking at the grossest prospects. Not Louie, who picks his nose and eats it, or Zeke, who always farts, or Wesley, who walks like he has a stick up his butt.

Ardith says she wants one nice, smart guy who doesn't party or try to go up her shirt on the first date. Oh, and he has to have decent feet.

You want to date a *lot* of guys, be wined, dined, and romanced, and you want them all to think you're the hottest girl in the world. And you don't want anyone who hates dogs.

When the imagining shifts to sharing secrets, you confess that when you're alone at night you strain to separate the house's normal creaks and groans from the stealthy approach of burglars and rapists. Sometimes you can tell the difference and sometimes you can't. When you can't, you curl up in the closet with Wendy's plaid blanket and a serrated steak knife from the kitchen.

"I keep a screwdriver under my pillow," Ardith says, shrugging. "Biggest, pointiest mother I could find. I'm not taking any chances."

"Would you actually use it?" you say, prying off your Nikes. "I mean, you said your house is always full of people. Couldn't you just scream for help?"

"I could," she says, "but look who'd show up."

Later in the week, you and Ardith each add a new claw hammer to your arsenals.

September rolls around. Ninth grade starts and the days whip by. Your parents come home from work early on Fridays now and take you out to dinner, shepherding you into the same crowded, upscale restaurant week after week, smiling as they sip wine and occasionally touch hands. They ask about school, teachers, homework, and friends, hanging on your every word and only shifting attention when colleagues stop to say hello.

"That went very well," your mother says on the first night during the ride home, when you're slumped in the back of your father's Lexus, woozy from too much food and attention. "We'll do this every Friday. I'll make a standing reservation."

"Every Friday?" your father says, braking for a red light. "For how long?"

"For as long as it takes," your mother says coolly, shaking back her hair.

The light turns green. Your father sighs and accelerates.

"It's important to present a united front, especially in public," your mother says, giving him a pointed look.

"I know," he mutters, turning into the cul-de-sac. "I don't need a lecture."

"Fine," she says, gathering her purse. "But next week keep your wine consumption down to two glasses and your attention on your daughter when she speaks. Glazed eyes and fidgeting don't exactly indicate rapt fascination, you know."

"I'm doing my best," your father says through gritted teeth.

"Well, do better," your mother replies. "Important people are watching."

You sit like a stone as your father cruises up your driveway and straight into the garage. The overhead door closes behind you. You climb out of the plush backseat and follow your bickering parents into the house.

Your mother stops you on the way to your room.

"Oh, and next week, Blair, don't shovel your pasta in like you're eating with a trowel," she says, unbuttoning her jacket. "It's not necessary to finish everything on your plate, either. It makes you look . . . starved." She tugs her silk blouse out of her waistband. "And try to keep the 'you knows' and 'likes' down to a minimum, please. You're conversing with adults now, not classmates." She pushes your hair from your eyes and studies your face. Her fingers are cool and smooth. "Taming this mop is next and then we really do have to do something about your wardrobe. Remind me, will you?" She sails off to her room, mistaking your silence for agreement.

You lay awake that night, watching Wendy's urn glitter in the moonlight, and rubbing your stomach as the ziti burns high into your throat.

You told them about your classes and teachers. Babbled on, hogged the conversation, even shared some of the cleaner jokes going around school. The more they listened, chuckled, and exchanged proud-parent looks, the more you talked yourself into believing they were truly interested.

You burp. Exhale scalding breath.

You must not *really* have believed them, though, because when they asked about your friends, you didn't tell them about Ardith. No, a colleague interrupted that question and for some reason, maybe instinct, you allowed it to pass unanswered.

And they must not have really cared, because they let it pass, too.

With the exception of Happy Family Fridays, your lifestyle makes it easy to keep secrets.

Ardith comes home with you after school, eating over, doing

homework, strolling down to Dunkin Donuts with the dogged hope of running into Officer Dave, and then leaving at ten, right before one or both of your parents is scheduled to arrive.

You treat Ardith to dinner at Chili's for her birthday and then the two of you go to your first Thanksgiving dance as ninth graders, the oldest kids in junior high. You slow dance with anyone who asks, just to get the feel of it. By the time the night is over, your arms have been draped around five different necks and your shirt is spotted from five pairs of damp hands.

Ardith has danced with only one guy, Jeremy, but they danced three times and he took her phone number.

"You know what was weird?" you say, pondering this interesting new power you have to make guys sweat. "They were all so nervous. I mean, they danced with me but they wouldn't even look at me."

"You're too intense," Ardith says, wearing the same vague, moony smile she's sported all evening. "Jeremy says you're like an extreme sport."

"What? Why?" You're peeved at his intrusion into your conversation, but also intrigued by the unexpected opportunity to hear a guy's opinion of you. And you don't think it's at all strange that your best friend and the guy she likes spent their dance time discussing *you*. You think it's excellent.

"Jeremy goes mountain climbing with his dad," Ardith says, pulling a pack of cigarettes from her coat pocket. You each take one and glance over your shoulders, making sure the coast is clear before lighting up.

"So what does that have to do with me?" you say, exhaling a hearty stream of smoke. It's too windy to blow rings.

"That's what *I* said, and he laughed and said the first time you check out a mountain, it's like this awesome challenge but you're pretty sure you can handle it," she says, flicking her ashes. "But when you get up close and see what you're *really* taking on, you still have to climb it because you already told everybody you would. So you do, but you're scared and sweating your ass off, hoping that if you just keep going and don't think, you'll make it through." She grins. "When you're done, you either quit climbing forever or the rush sends you right back for more."

"And the mountain is supposed to be me," you say, and lapse into contemplative silence for the rest of the walk home. You skip up your driveway, deciding that if Ardith likes Jeremy, he must be pretty smart. And you hope for her sake that he has decent feet.

Your parents bite the togetherness bullet, and you spend Thanksgiving Day three hours away at your grandmother's, ignoring the indifference in your father's voice when he talks to your mother and the dagger look she gives him when he excuses himself during dinner to make an important phone call.

Your grandmother says the turkey is dry and the mashed potatoes lumpy because dinner was ready an hour before you arrived. If you had just called on that fancy cell phone to say you would be late, well, then maybe the cranberry sauce would still be chilled and the turnips hot.

Your grandfather wears a bib and eats with his fingers. He washes his mashed potatoes in his apple cider like a gaunt, senile raccoon and then searches his hands, wondering where his food has gone.

You eat two helpings of potatoes and three of turnips while studying the egg-headed, papier-mâché, yarn-haired angels your grandmother relentlessly crafts and imprisons in the china cabinet. They crowd the glass, staring out with vacant, unblinking eyes and beseeching with knotted, pipe cleaner hands. Their feathered wings are molting and their robes sparkle with the fallen glitter from their sisters' halos. Redhead, blonde, brunette; their smooth, unsmiling faces all look disturbingly alike and you wish your grandmother would go back to decoupaging Norman Rockwell scenes onto old pickle jars instead.

"Give me your hand." Your grandmother captures your grandfather's arm and wipes the smeary mashed potatoes from between his fingers. "There now, isn't that better?" She looks at your father. "I had to change his shirt twice before you got here. The first time, he pulled the giblets out of the bag and emptied them into his pocket. Then, he—"

"Is he always this bad?" your mother interrupts.

"We're getting along just fine," your grandmother says, avoiding her gaze.

Your mother leans forward in her chair. "Mother, if he's becoming unmanageable, he belongs in a home."

"God, Mom," you mutter. "He's not *deaf.*"

"Eat your dinner," your mother says without even glancing your way.

"He's my husband," your grandmother says.

"And *my* father," your mother shoots back.

"May I have the peas?" your father says pleasantly, as if your mother hasn't just wrenched the lid off an enormous can of worms and dashed them across the dinner table.

"He may as well not be anyone's father, for all the attention he gets from you," your grandmother says, taking the spoon from your grandfather, turning it right side up, and handing it back to him. "It'd break his heart to know that his only daughter is too busy making money to come and see him."

Your mother bristles. "I have to earn a living, Mother. Isn't that why you sent me to college? So I'd have a career to fall back on if my husband ever left me?" She thrusts the bowl of peas into your father's hands. "So I wouldn't have to send my daughter to the store with food stamps while my husband is out whoring around with his secretary?"

"Butter, please," your father says, forcing a smile.

No one moves, so you reach across the table and hand it over. The knife rattles against the silver-plated dish during the brief transfer.

"And now you want me to jeopardize *my* security and *my* career for a man who walked out on us without a second thought?" Her anger sucks the oxygen from the room.

"He came back," your grandmother says, covering your grandfather's hand with her own gnarled one. "He missed us and he came back."

"He came *back* because she dumped him when he lost his job." Your mother flings the words like jagged-edged stones. "He came *back* because he had nowhere else to go and you let him. He *hurt* us—"

"That was thirty years ago," your grandmother says.

"That was *yesterday*!" your mother cries, slamming her hand down on the table. "He doesn't remember it and you don't want to, but *I do*."

No one moves. You stare at your plate, thinking of what you've just learned and what you already know. You don't want to understand it.

"Hey," your father says finally. "How 'bout that Tiger Woods?"

Your grandfather farts. "I poofed," he whispers, hunching his shoulders.

"He belongs in a care facility," your mother says stiffly and her eyes widen as the unmistakable scent of a bowel movement penetrates the air. "Oh, for Christ's sake, Mother! He just went to the bathroom in his pants!"

"It's all right," your grandmother soothes, taking your grandfather's quivering arm and helping him to his feet. "No harm done, Stanley. Let's clean you up." And to my father, "He wears those adult diapers now, so it's much easier than it was." She puts her arm around his waist and gently leads him out.

"So," your father says grimly, leaning back in his chair and smoothing his tie, "would you mind telling me what you were hoping to accomplish with that? Other than making the rest of us wish we were elsewhere, of course."

"Shut up," your mother says, pushing away her plate and fanning the air. Her cheeks are red and her gaze distracted. "This is a fiasco. I had no idea he was this bad. She should have warned me. We wouldn't have come." Her fanning increases. "He's draining the life out of her all over again."

"That's her choice," your father says, shrugging. "You can't change it."

"Maybe not, but I don't have to sit here and watch it happen," your mother says, caught up in an argument that will never end.

"True, and your mother doesn't need the stress of company on top of everything else," your father says, which is the closest he's come to agreeing with her all day. "Tell you what; let's facilitate this whole affair. You and Blair clear the plates and I'll get the coffee going." He tosses his crumpled, paper Thanksgiving napkin on the table and rises.

You look at the goofy, cartoon turkey on the soiled napkin and then past it at the old, white lace tablecloth. It's been mended so many times the scars are part of the pattern. You think of your grandmother, sitting in her recliner with the cloth on her lap, head bent and fingers cramped from the tiny, even stitches, and of your puzzled, blank-eyed grandfather, shaking your hand when you came in, asking your name and saying it was nice to meet you.

You think of hollow, fragile angels trapped in a glass cage and Norman Rockwell families painstakingly collected, layered, and shellacked onto empty jars. You think of Wendy that last morning before you left for school, of letting her out to pee, brushing off her ever-hopeful request to play, and leaving her with a quick pat and the promise of a nice long walk when you got home.

Only when you got home, it was already too late.

"Well?" your mother says, reaching for your plate.

"I'm not done yet," you say, and take another heaping spoonful of mashed potatoes and two more shivering, ruby slices of cranberry sauce.

"Well, pack it up and take it with you," your father says impatiently.

You pick up your fork and begin cutting the cranberry sauce into bite-size pieces.

"Blair, didn't you hear what your father just said?" your mother asks.

"I'm hungry *now*," you say, forcing one of the slippery wedges into your mouth. The truth is that you're not hungry at all, but you've just realized you never needed to tell your grandmother that Grandpa couldn't come to the new house because he was incontinent. The truth is that she knew it all along.

"That's your third helping of potatoes," your father says.

"They're good," you say as your grandmother escorts your freshly dressed grandfather back into the room.

"They're lumpy," she says automatically, but for a second light shines in her eyes and you know she's pleased at your pleasure. She leads your grandfather to his chair and presses his shoulders until he sits. "Now, where were we?"

"We were talking about putting him in a nursing home," your mother says.

Your grandfather's head jerks up, his hand out and the plastic tumbler of cloudy, curdled cider tips over. Your grandmother runs for the paper towels, your father shakes his head, and your grandfather starts to weep. You put your napkin over the spill and pat his scarecrow arm and watch your mother ignore her father, and when the burning in your chest reaches critical mass, you say, "You know, Mom, Alzheimer's is hereditary," and smile as her detachment turns to bald horror.

You shovel in the rest of your food while the adults argue and when the shouting reaches its crescendo, you slip into the bathroom and, for the first time ever, stick your finger down your throat. Your stomach groans under the weight of your gluttony and, with effort, obeys your request and heaves up Thanksgiving.

When you finish retching you sit back on your heels, sweating, shaking, and feeling worse than you did before. Your mouth is sour, the stench sickening, and you can't even look at the mess in the toilet. Disgusted, you flush twice just to wash it all away.

You return to the table, eat a tiny piece of pumpkin pie and drink your coffee alone in the middle of the fray. Not long after that, you accept the tray of leftovers your grandmother slaps together. You hug your grandfather good-bye and tell him it was nice meeting him. He draws back and looks at you like you're crazy.

Your grandmother hugs you and struggles to say something, but never finds the words. You tell her you're glad the lace tablecloth is a family tradition. Your father beeps the horn and you almost give him the finger. Instead, you climb into the back of the Lexus and wave until your grandparents are out of sight.

You father glances across the front seat at your mother. "For the record, I won't sit through another dinner like that." He merges into highway traffic and glides, without signaling, over to the fast lane.

"Don't worry, I won't ask you to," she says, staring out the passenger window.

You wonder who'll mend the tablecloth when your grandmother dies and realize no one will. It'll be thrown out because it's imperfect and a pain to take care of.

You close your eyes and simmer in silence.

Chapter 6

Ardith

You know what I like about you?

You get it. You *understand*. You're not laying there going, "Oh right, poor little rich Blair; what does she have to complain about?" or saying her parents only work hard so she can have nice things. That's crap, and I'm glad you know it. Most people don't.

Blair's Thanksgiving was better than mine. I know how that sounds, but it's true. My parents are weird about holidays—we can't go out, everyone has to come to us—so I was stuck in the house all day. Not that I had anywhere to go, but still.

The two-minute highlight was when Jeremy called. The bad part was that he called during halftime, when my brother's stupid friends had abandoned the TV and were in the kitchen scavenging for leftovers. I took the cordless phone into the living room just to stay out of their way, but a couple of them had to follow me, making kissing sounds and lewd comments.

Jeremy got all tense and said, "Guess I called at a bad time."

"No," I said. "They're just—"

"Yeah, well, later," he said and hung up.

Click.

I freaked. I did. I came out swinging and managed to bash the receiver into the closest head before they pinned me and clamped their hands over my mouth to keep me from hollering down the house. I kicked, bit, and went into total, writhing wild-thing mode until my mother came in and told everyone the game was back on.

They left.

She stayed, sipping her cosmopolitan.

I sat up. My nose was bleeding.

"So cookie, what was that all about?" she said, handing me a tissue.

"They ruined it," I said hoarsely, jamming the tissue up my nostril. My hands were shaking and I was one step away from bawling. "That was somebody important and they were making disgusting comments and now he'll never call again."

"Well, it's his loss," my mother said, shrugging. "Screw him if he can't take a joke, right?" She smiled, smoothed the hair from my sweaty forehead, and drained her drink. "Go clean up, baby, and we'll bring out the pumpkin pie. Your father's tapping a keg and if we don't keep the food coming, these gorillas will tear the place apart."

So I did, but the fights broke out anyway between rival football fans with big mouths. I escaped to my room right after the guy with the phone dent shoved my father. Gil went backward over an ottoman and whacked his head on the coffee table.

My brother broke it up, but my father was left with a wicked, four-day headache and my mother charged everyone twenty bucks a piece to clean the mess out of the carpet.

When I went back to school, Jeremy wouldn't even look at me. Within a week he was holding hands with Kimmer Ashton.

Lirgas. Right.

I'm feeling a little sick right now, so I'll let Blair start on Christmas.

Chapter 7

Blair

Ardith said she was sick? Yeah, that'd be about right, considering what we're leading up to.

Christmas. High hopes, stupid expectations. Brutal reality.

The decorators put up a massive fake tree in the living room. They hung a wreath on the door, garland up the banister, tapestry stockings on the mantel, and white-bulb candles in the windows.

A mailing firm sent out our Christmas cards. My mother's personal shopper delivered eleven bags of wrapped and tagged presents. Lourdes hummed "Jingle Bell Rock," prepared the seafood for Christmas Eve dinner, and set our dining room table.

No one played carols, made cookies, or stuffed the stockings. Grandma and Grandpa weren't penciled into my parents' social calendars, as they had done their duty and visited on Thanksgiving.

Christmas was better in the old house.

Oh, for only a thousand reasons.

Every year we'd go down to the farmer's market on Christmas Eve and buy one of the scrawny, leftover Charlie Brown trees that nobody else wanted because they had bare spots or weren't perfectly symmetrical. My parents would always make like we were going to buy a big, fluffy balsam or a blue spruce instead, but I wouldn't budge.

You know why? It sounds kind of dumb now, but I read a story once about a perfect little fir tree that opened its branches to shelter all the birds and animals in the forest during a terrible blizzard. It kept them safe, but because its branches were open, instead of closed tight like all the other trees, the storm battered the little fir pretty badly.

Afterward everyone thought the little fir was too broken and ugly to take home and decorate for Christmas, so they just left it there in the forest, imperfect and alone.

You know what? I don't even remember how the story ends, but I never wanted a perfect tree after reading it and I don't think I ever will.

Yeah, Save the Charlie Brown Trees. That's me. Wise guy.

Anyway, when we got home, my father would make spiced cider while my mother and I sang "O Christmas Tree," strung the lights, and hung the ornaments. Wendy would be everywhere, sniffing, prancing, rooting her stocking out of the box . . . and, oh God, this was so funny. Every time we bent over she would nose our butts, just to make us jump. She loved Christmas so much . . .

Wait.

Okay. No. I'm all right now.

On Christmas Eve, once I was supposedly in bed, my father would always give my mother some kind of lacy nightie or lingerie. They would sit on the couch and he'd watch while she opened the gift box, like he wanted to be sure she really loved it. She'd admire it and then kiss him and that's when I would sneak back to bed. I used to think, *Ugh, who wants to see their parents kissing?* But now . . .

I don't know exactly why it stopped, but I *do* know that the same year my mother gave up her private practice and joined this big law firm, instead of them staying up for the lingerie gift like usual, they just shut off the tree lights and went to bed.

It's so weird, how everything changed after that. I mean, you'd think my father would have been happy that more money was coming in, but instead he got, like, resentful that she wasn't there to make dinner or get his dry cleaning or whatever. There was this tension between them that just kept getting worse, until all they did was, like, *pick* at each other. It was horrible.

And then came stupid Amber, but I really don't want to think about her anymore.

Yeah, I'm fine. Let me just tell the rest of the story.

Where was I? Oh, Christmas in the new house.

We ate in the dining room on Christmas Eve, the three of us seated at a mahogany table built for twelve. There were vanilla-scented candles, a poinsettia centerpiece, and a gold tablecloth with matching china, glass, and flatware. Anyone glancing in through the sheer drapes would see a family gathered together in picturesque celebration.

"That's your third drink," my mother said, watching my father pour another neat Johnnie Walker Black. "We're going to midnight mass tonight, remember?"

"How could I forget?" he muttered and downed it in one gulp. "The place will probably go up in flames the minute we set foot inside."

"Don't be ridiculous," my mother said, snapping a snow crab

leg in half and tweezing out the slender stalk of meat. "It's never too late to practice your faith."

"Especially among an influential congregation," my father said dryly, refilling his glass. "A toast: To goals attained and a speedy appointment to the bench. May justice prevail." He laughed, drank, choked, and left the table coughing.

I tore the crusts off my grilled cheese sandwich and set them aside to throw out for the birds. Their motives were pure—hunger, thirst, shelter—and they didn't mind leftovers.

My mother focused on me. "What're you eating? What kind of holiday meal is that? Since when do you prefer sandwiches to seafood?" She ripped the shrimp's body from its tail and dropped the empty shell onto the pile on her plate.

I shrugged. I hadn't eaten dead fish or animals since I was twelve, but pointing that out would only piss her off, and she was already revved up enough to run me over.

My father returned, took his seat, and resumed eating. He noticed my mother's censorious look and draped his cloth napkin across his lap.

We finished in silence and moved to the living room to open gifts.

"Oh, how lovely," my mother said, lifting a cultured pearl necklace from a Tiffany's box. "It's absolutely perfect."

"Who gave you that?" my father asked.

"You did," she said coolly.

The personal shopper must have had strict instructions from my mother, because all my gifts were clothes, the kind of expensive, boring, tailored outfits adults love seeing kids wear because it reflects well on them.

My father gave my mother a check and me a cell phone.

I was forced to wear one of my new outfits to mass, a taupe one so bland that I faded into the Wraith of Christmas Present.

St. Anthony's Church was all oak and glass, modern and chilly. My mother said its congregation was the cream of the crop. She lingered in the vestibule to meet some of them afterward, including Dr. Luna, a prominent plastic surgeon, his county freeholder wife, and their daughter.

"Dellasandra is right around your age, Blair," my mother said, smiling and giving me an eyeball nudge in the girl's direction.

"Oh?" My mother must have been delirious because there was no way this short, sparkly girl drenched in plush, ruby velvet was fourteen. Her huge boobs and dark, shimmering, waist-length hair clocked her in at fifteen minimum.

"Hi." Dellasandra squirmed around my father to stand next to me. "Did you hear the soloist burp when she was singing 'Ave Maria'? I almost laughed, but I didn't want to hurt her feelings. How old are you?" She tucked her hair behind her ear, exposing a pea-size diamond stud, but her fingers were short and stubby, the nails chewed down to nubs.

"Fifteen, next week," I said as an off-duty altar boy squeezed by, trailing the sharp scent of incense. He goggled at Dellasandra, but I was a giant, taupe blind spot.

"And how old do you think *I* am?" she asked, almost before I finished speaking. "Here, wait." She squared her shoulders and smoothed her dress.

The hourglass motion sent the altar boy reeling out into the night.

"Okay. *Now* guess." Dellasandra's eyes were squirrel bright.

I hesitated. Something was weird here. Her body screamed *Girls*

Gone Wild but her manner was way Barney. All quivery, kiddie, I've-got-a-secret excitement.

"C'mon, guess!" she said and it wasn't a request.

Annoyed, I decided not to award her the compliment of driving age. "I don't know," I said, shrugging. "Fifteen?"

"Wrong!" she crowed, laughing and twirling around. "I'm twelve!"

"Hey, tone it down there, enchantress," her father said, giving her hair a gentle tug. "We're still in church, remember?"

Giggling, she clapped a hand over her mouth. "Sorry, Daddy." Her hair swung out as she turned back to me. "I do that all the time. Get too loud, I mean. My mother says it's because I'm home-schooled and used to being the center of attention, but I don't think that's accurate. I think some of us are just naturally filled with joie de vivre. That means 'joy of living,' just in case you didn't know. Isn't that a great phrase? I know lots more. I have a really high IQ. I'm studying French and Spanish, and by the time I graduate I'll know Japanese and Russian, too. I'd make a great UN ambassador, don't you think? Except my mother says I lack social skills and need to attend a real school so I can expose myself to a wide variety of people and situations."

Expose herself? A snort of laughter escaped.

"What?" Dellasandra cried, pouncing and clutching my arm. "Tell me."

I shook my head and covered my mouth, but another snicker erupted.

"Are you laughing at me?" Her fingers tugged and pinched, but to no avail. She turned to her mother, who was talking to my father, and interrupted by dragging on her arm. "Mom, she's laughing and won't tell me why."

"Blair," my mother warned in a deadly undertone.

"Blair's just having fun," her mother said, stroking her daughter's hair. "It's late and people get giddy." She glanced at her Rolex. "Ten past, everyone. Merry Christmas!"

The hint was taken and we cordially disbursed, Dellasandra tucked between her parents, me trailing along behind mine.

I expected to catch shit for irking the *enchantress*, but all my mother said when we were in the car was, "The Lunas are the single-most influential connection I've made so far, Blair, and I expect to strengthen the relationship. Camella Luna is no fan of the crew in the prosecutor's office, thank God, and she's a *very* strong voice in the political arena. Her support will be invaluable. I'm hoping you and Dellasandra will become good friends."

I'd known it was coming, so I nodded a lie and she turned back to the front, pleased that her puppet would perform.

When I woke up on Christmas day, no one was home and wouldn't be for quite a while. The note on the counter was a list of VIP gala holiday events that extended throughout the week, beginning in Manhattan and consistently moving north until finally culminating in a New Year's Day grand finale up at Martha's Vineyard.

My mother had apparently forgotten that Lourdes was on vacation. I mulled it over and, despite the unrelenting silence, decided not to call and remind her.

I smoked in the kitchen. Gagged on my father's Johnnie Walker Black. Programmed my new cell phone.

And called Ardith, who was also in holiday hell.

Chapter 8

Ardith's Story

Your father spends the day in a fake fur Santa hat and a cheesy white beard that makes his lips look like calf's liver. He ho-ho-hos and drags every passing female down onto his lap for a shot of Peppermint Schnapps and a candy cane.

You avoid being caught under the mistletoe by sculpting a lumpy, red cold sore at the edge of your mouth with clotted concealer and lipstick, then slathering it with chalky white Blistex. You wear an Albert Einstein T-shirt, lime green sweats, and pink quilted bedroom booties. The pictures will be gruesome but if this doesn't exclude you from the slap-n-tickle line, then nothing will.

Your parents ignore your wish list of books about foot massage and podiatry and give you makeover software, a flowered kimono, henna tattoos, ribbed tops, Britney's cologne, lipstick, and a gold ankle bracelet.

When the unwrapping is done, you tote your gifts into your bedroom to be divvied up between the Macy's return counter and

Blair. She'll love the software, tops, and ankle bracelet; ever since she found out Jeremy called you over Thanksgiving she's been on a boyfriend quest and will not be denied. She doesn't understand it yet, but she's way too potent for ninth graders.

By midafternoon, when Blair calls for the third time and makes you feel guilty for not inviting her over, your father's half-lit, your brother's bored, and your mother's Frederick's of Hollywood Santa's helper costume is showing a scary amount of cleavage. The cosmos have been replaced with spiked eggnog and the keg squats in the corner like a resident troll.

You don't want to bring Blair here, but she's lonesome and you're not allowed out today, so you surrender and issue the dreaded invitation.

"Dress ugly," you tell her. "Wear the biggest, baggiest clothes you own. No makeup. Eat an onion. This house is full of drunks and they're gonna be all over you anyway, so don't show up looking like a toothsome morsel."

Blair laughs, and when she arrives with your presents, her eyes are sparkling and her color is high. She's wearing a funky pair of black, stretch-velvet, low-rise flares and a sheer, red, baby-doll top that ends right above her belly button. Black satin platforms shoot her up to around five feet eleven and a thick, gold cuff bracelet encircles her wrist.

"You're dead, you know," you say, shaking your head as she laughs, flustered and glowing at the guys crowding around her.

"Who *is* that?" your mother says, frowning.

"A girl from school," you say, watching as the guys hustle her to the mistletoe hanging in the doorway between the TV room and the kitchen. Your brother is first, Broken Nose and Phone Dent impatient at the back of the line.

"Well, don't plan on hanging around with her," your mother says, shifting and deliberately blocking your father's pop-eyed stare. "You don't need to get involved with a boy-crazy girl like that. She acts like a little whore." Muttering, she refills her eggnog tumbler and settles on your father's lap, preventing him from joining the fest. The other girls look sullen and you begin to think you'd better get Blair away before a fight erupts.

Before you can move, Broken Nose slips his hand up under Blair's shirt and squeezes her breast.

Shocked, she pushes it away. Slaps his other hand from her butt. A terrible mix of little-girl confusion and big-girl outrage twists her face. She says, "C'mon now, quit it," but her voice is wobbly and her smile smashed as he kisses her. Someone cheers as his tongue invades her mouth.

You look at your mother, who shrugs and says, "Well, she asked for it."

At your father, who looks like he wishes she'd asked *him* for it, and at your brother, who watches with undisguised interest.

"Break it up," you yell, but no one pays any attention.

Your mother elbows your father. "You know what, Gil? We should do some dirty dancing. I have the CD here somewhere. It'd be fun."

Your father grunts, his gaze locked on the floor show.

You go into the kitchen. Turn on the stove and dip the festive Rudolph kitchen towel into the flickering flames. It ignites. You hold it up beneath the smoke detector, loosing an endless, ear-splitting shriek and scattering the cringing, reeling crowd.

Blair stumbles toward you, lipstick smeared and clothes askew. You toss the burning towel into the sink and lead her into your room. Lock the door.

She drops onto your bed, hands fluttering and twisting in her lap like broken-winged birds. Her face is pale, her eyes huge.

You point to her breast so she can pop it back into its lace cup.

"Holy shit," she says, rearranging herself. "Oh my *God*, what the hell was that? What does he think I am? I can't believe it. Why didn't your parents do something?"

What answer can you give? Because any girl who comes into this house is automatically fair game? Because your mother thought Blair deserved what she got? Because your father would have been first, front and center, had he been able to get up? Any or all of the above?

"I'm so freaked," she says, kicking off her platforms and pacing the room. "I mean, I know you said to look ugly, but God, I wanted to look good for Christmas and yeah, okay, so maybe I was hoping I'd get kissed, but not like *that*." She sinks down on the bed. "Not like *that* at all."

You don't say anything, not even "I told you so," because you know she never really understood your home life anyway. But you think it and somewhere in the darkest corner of your mind, a small, spiteful voice whispers, *Well, she asked for it,* and is pleased because now you two aren't so different after all.

You stifle it, ashamed.

"I mean, everything was fine," she continues bewilderedly, rubbing her forehead. "You saw. They were joking and laughing and just, like, pecking my mouth. Nothing big. Nothing bad. And then that last guy . . ."

"Broken Nose," you say.

"Whatever. He ruined it." She runs her nails across her velvet pants, disturbing the nap. "He made it disgusting." She peeks at you through tangled hair. "Did he ever do that to you?"

"Once," you say and your fist throbs with the memory of crunching cartilage. Word spread quickly following his bloody, yowling exodus and only the real drunks are still brave—or stupid—enough to try and touch you in passing anymore.

Still, it never hurts to keep your guard up.

"He's a jerk," she says, slumping against your headboard and closing her eyes. "I don't like him at all."

"Me, either," you say, perching on the edge of the bed. You're not sure what else to say because you're not sure what she's thinking. You have an idea, though, and you want very badly to be wrong.

Minutes pass.

"God, he went right up under my shirt in front of everybody," she says without opening her eyes. Her arms, which are folded tightly across her chest, relax and settle lower, with her hands loosely tented over her belly button. "The others weren't bad. They didn't touch me or anything." She's reliving it in her mind, weighing, sorting, still searching for the keys to an unfamiliar kingdom. "I mean, I can't hate them *all* for what one of them did." She cracks an eye. "Right?"

Your stomach sinks.

"That wouldn't be fair," she says, opening the other eye and sitting up straight. "It'd be kind of like stereotyping, don't you think? Condemning everyone just because one person did wrong?"

You know what she wants to hear, but you just can't say it, so you say this instead: "I've only seen them in a herd," you say carefully. "Maybe one-on-one they're different. It's possible, I guess. I don't know. But I wouldn't count on it."

"Well, it doesn't make any difference, because they all probably think I'm disgusting now anyway," she says, sighing.

"Actually, they're so blitzed they probably won't even remember you," you say to comfort her and are surprised to see hurt stain her face. "I mean, this is kind of an everyday affair around here." Somehow you seem to be twisting the knife. "Although they *did* get more carried away with you than they normally do."

Her eyes light up. "Really? So you don't think they'd forget me?"

"No," you say, surrendering as she rises and goes to the mirror. "But—"

"This *is* a good outfit," she says, twisting sideways and patting her abdomen. She leans close and examines her face. "God, look what he did to my makeup." She plucks a tissue from the box and scrubs the red smears from her bruised mouth. "Do you think he's sorry?"

"No," you say. "I think he'd do it again in a heartbeat, given the chance."

"Well, then, I'll just have to stay away from him, won't I?" she says, studying her reflection. She unwinds her wrist bag and spills her makeup across the bureau's cluttered surface. "How old are the others? Who was the first one?"

"Most of them are around eighteen," you say dully, watching as she applies a fresh, glossy coat of scarlet lipstick. "The first guy who kissed you was my brother."

"Really?" she says, turning away from the bureau. "You never told me your brother was hot." She bends and brushes her hair forward. "He's eighteen?"

"*Going* on eighteen," you say. "He'll be a senior when we're sophomores."

"So my first real kiss came from a seventeen-year-old," she says.

"Who's already seeing somebody," you say, disturbed by the lilt in her voice.

"Think he'd dump her for me?" she says, standing upright and flipping back her hair. It falls in glorious, glistening waves down past her shoulders and she hams it up, planting a hand on her hip and batting her eyelashes at you.

You don't respond and her mischief falls away.

"Ardith, he gave me this really intense look right before he kissed me," she says, dropping next to you on the bed and clutching your knee. "I mean, *really* intense, like he'd been looking for me his whole life, you know? Like he really *saw* me."

She makes you want to cry. Or scream. Or just turn away and shout, "Go ahead then! You won't listen to me, so go find out for yourself!"

"And he wasn't grabby or anything," she says, her gaze going dreamy. "He just gave this sexy little sigh and placed this gentle, gentle Christmas kiss on my lips . . ."

"He's a dog, Blair," you say flatly. "A total player."

"Maybe not," she says, releasing your knee. "You said yourself that everybody's different when they're one-on-one—"

"Yeah, but he's not better different, he's worse different," you say.

"How do *you* know?" she says, pulling away and staring at you. "What if he *does* like me? What if he's serious, not like those jerkoffs from the dance who never even called! God, why is it so hard to believe that someone might actually want to be with me? Am I really that much of a loser?"

You meet her raw gaze and struggle for words to heal the sudden wound between you. "No, I'm sorry. I swear that's not what I meant. *You're* not the loser, *he* is, and I just don't want him to hurt you—"

Your apology is interrupted by a knock on the door.

"What?" you snarl.

"Open up for a minute, Ardith."

It's him, your brother, and you make the hideous and final mistake of saying so.

"Oh my God," Blair whispers, eyes shining. She clutches your arm and the fight is forgiven. Everything will be forgiven, provided you open the door. "What if he fell madly in love with me and wants to ask me out? Quick! No, wait. Let me look good first."

"Don't," you say but she isn't listening. She's busy posing on the bed, stretching out on her side and propping her head up on her elbow.

He knocks again, louder.

Blair gives you a pleading look.

No, you want to say. *I won't. Go ahead and be mad, I don't care.* But instead you look away feeling old, sick, and tarnished, because you know you're going to do it. You're going to give her what she thinks she wants, surrender to her rosy naïveté, and in doing so, to that spiteful, maybe even jealous voice inside of you that whispers, *Well, she asked for it.* You're going to do it, and you wish you were dead.

"Don't let him leave, Ardith," she whispers. "Please?"

"Who's out there with you?" you ask before you open the door. If the mob stampedes, you have no flaming torches left to fight them off.

"Just me," he says impatiently. "Open up."

You do, reluctantly, and he's alone. His beery exhales sting your nose.

"Connie's pissed because you almost burned down the kitchen," he says, but not to you. His gaze is riveted on Blair, who ignores him and fluffs her hair.

"You know why I did it," you say. "Things got out of control."

"Hey, don't blame me for what those idiots do," he says, smiling as Blair glances at him. "Me, I see a fine hottie standing under the mistletoe and I want to be with her, sure, but I also want to give her the respect she deserves."

"Gee, I'll tell your girlfriend you said so," you say sarcastically, earning a frown from Blair and an irritated look from your brother.

"So anyhow, wiseass, Connie says Christmas is a family holiday and company has to go home," he says, leaning against the door-jamb.

"All the company or just mine?" you say, already knowing the answer. Fate is conspiring against you and you can't fight a battle no one wants you to win.

"Beats me," he drawls, smiling at Blair to show no hard feelings. "Why don't you go ask her yourself?"

You glance at Blair and she sends you a silent, eyeball *okay,* but it doesn't make you feel any better, so you don't go. Instead you say, "If nobody else is leaving, then Blair's not leaving, either."

"Wait. Connie's your mother, right?" Blair asks, sitting up. Her stomach pooches a little over her pants and you can tell your brother likes that; he prefers his babes built for comfort, not speed.

"Right," he says, letting his gaze linger on her bare stomach until he's sure she's noticed, then easing it up to her face.

"Oh God, well, if your mother says I should leave," she says, blushing and reaching for her shoes.

"It's too cold to walk," he says, crouching in front of her and doing the Cinderella's glass slippper thing, which makes you want to barf. "I'll drive you home."

Her spontaneous smile is nuclear and your brother actually flinches before he disappears in the blinding, white light. He reappears, dazed. "I, uh, well, okay, uh, I guess I'll pick you up out front."

"I'm coming, too," you say.

"No you're not," he says, right as she blurts, "You don't have to, Ardith. I mean, I don't want you to get in trouble with your mom."

You give her a look and she gives you one back that comes with a tossed head and a stubborn chin.

You shrug. "Fine. Whatever." You leave and wait for your brother near the kitchen. "You'd better not do anything to her," you say when he comes out jingling his car keys.

He smirks and keeps walking.

"I mean it," you say, darting around and blocking his path. It's a good way to die but you barely care. "God, why can't you just leave her alone? There are five other girls here you could be with—"

"Been there, done that," he says and shoves you aside.

"But you don't understand. She's *fourteen*, she's never even had a boyfriend before," you say desperately, dogging his footsteps and hoping Blair never gets wind of your treachery. "Don't do anything to her, do you hear me?" You've crossed the line but you'd be no kind of friend if you didn't make one last, futile attempt. *"Don't."*

You go back to your room, where Blair is practicing come-hither looks in the mirror. If she uses one on him, she'll never be the same again. "Blair—"

"I left your presents on the bed," she chirps. "I'll call you later." She laughs and the air crackles. "Some Christmas so far, huh?"

"Yeah." You hand her a small, wrapped box and she wedges it into her bag. Her wrists are so thin and easy to snap. "Don't trust him, okay? Don't let him in."

"Don't worry about me. You just watch out for that jerk in your TV room," she says, beaming and sweeping out.

You stand at the living room window. Watch your brother open the Nissan's passenger door and help Blair in. Someone comes up beside you. It's the girl he's seeing.

"He's such an asshole," she says, watching the car back out of the driveway and rumble off down the street.

"Yup," you say, because this isn't exactly news.

She exhales on the windowpane and draws a star in the false fog. "I'm probably gonna break up with him when he gets back. I mean, this isn't the first time he's cheated on me."

"He's just giving her a ride," you say, wishing she would go bother someone else.

"Right. The ride of her life." She balls her hand into a fist, hesitates, and uncurls her fingers. Her eyes fill with tears. "It's really hard being the one who loves the *most,* you know?" She waits a minute and when you don't answer, she sniffles and wanders back into the family room.

You gaze at her window artwork for a moment, then wipe it away.

Your brother doesn't deserve that kind of longing.

Especially now that he's messing with Blair.

You should have stopped this. You should have flattened his tires, drugged his beer, or locked him in the cellar, anything to have kept them apart. You never should have invited her over, never brought her into his warped orbit.

Stupid, stupid.

You call Blair's cell phone and get voice mail. The same with her house phone. You try three more times, but can't get through and you don't know if that's good or bad. Maybe Blair's mother called and will talk so long that your brother will get tired of waiting and leave.

Oh God, if only.

It's impossible to sit still, so you reach for Blair's gifts and lose yourself in the four beautiful, user-friendly podiatry books. By the time you resurface, your brother's been gone for almost an hour.

Shit.

You change into jeans, pull on your coat, and slip out the door. It's cold and the streets are deserted. The sky is leaden, not yet dusk but no longer daylight.

Your brother's car is parked in Blair's driveway. You circle around the back of the house and peer into the family room through a crack in the miniblinds.

Clothes litter the floor. Your brother is sleeping, sprawled naked on the couch. His mouth is slack, his hair matted, and the soles of his feet are pink.

You shift, crunching skeletal, brown chrysanthemums beneath your boots.

Blair sits on the floor across from him. She pulls up her sleeve and lays her arm, splayed hand down, on the marble coffee table. Picks up a paring knife and drags the point across her forearm. Watches, hollow-eyed, as the blood wells.

"One," you think she says.

The chill rattles your bones. You stoop, pry a rock from the flower bed graveyard, and walk around the side of the house.

Pause in the shadows, gauge the distance, and fling the missile.

It bounces off the Nissan's hood and the silence is shattered by the car alarm.

You walk around to the back and watch through the blinds as your brother scrambles into his clothes, grabs his keys, and stumbles past Blair, who stares at the lone, scarlet rivulet trickling down the side of her forearm.

The look she gives his broad back is black with hatred.

She rises and walks after him, disappearing from view.

The car alarm stops and the ringing echoes fade. Blair returns, plops into a chair, and covers her face.

The Z's engine *vvrroooms* to life and rumbles away.

Your adrenaline ebbs and you slide down the wall between the bushes. Tilt your head back against the house and breathe hard, trying to get a grip. You saw too much, things you should never have seen, and you wonder if you should go to the door or just go home. You wonder if your brother had the brains to wear a condom and where you and Blair will get her abortion if he didn't.

You crouch there until your legs are numb and not even your armpits can warm your frigid hands, then rise and walk to the front door. You knock. Knock again and again.

You return to your window and peer inside. Blair is still huddled in the chair. You batter the glass and call her name until she lets you in.

I knew my brother would hurt Blair, I just didn't know how much, or exactly how to reverse the damage. Because that was my role now; turning what was left into more than just a pile of abandoned garbage.

No, I *know* she's not garbage. She never was. But that's how you feel when you realize you've been used. Totally worthless.

Yeah, I know I warned her, but she didn't want to believe me. No matter what you say, nobody ever believes it's going to happen to them.

So why should Blair be any different? Why should I?

Oh, we each have a blind spot. Mine just took a little longer to surface and level me. But we'll get to that.

This next part is Blair's.

Chapter 9

Blair's Story

You let Ardith in because you know she won't stop knocking until you do. Her face is pinched, her nose runny from the cold. Mingled with the concern in her eyes is a silent, damning "I told you so," and if she says it, you're going to cut yourself again, slash furrows down your whole arm so you never forget how stupid you feel.

You put the phone back on the hook, return to the armchair, and draw your knees up to your chest. Your thighs ache and your groin throbs. His invasion left slick, snail trails glistening across your skin and your nerves won't stop trying to twitch them away.

No sex ed class could ever have prepared you for what just happened.

"You've got a body that just don't quit, sweet thing," he says on the ride to your house. He drives too fast and pays more attention to you than to the road. It's scary but thrilling. The admiration in his voice dives straight into the pit of your stomach and smolders there. "You'd better get my sister to bring you around more often so I can see what I'm missing." His gaze lingers on your chest, lifts to your face. " 'Cause I've been missing a lot."

Your laugh is a shaky exhale because you know, right then, that he's going to come into your house and you're going to let him. He gave you your first real kiss, is spending his time and gas and no matter what Ardith says, he *must* like you because he left another girl behind on Christmas, just so you wouldn't have to walk home alone in the cold.

Heart pounding, you reach into your wrist bag and turn off your cell phone.

You're glad you were thrown out of Ardith's. Gladder still that you went over in the first place, because now you know what *you've* been missing, too.

"You warm enough?" he asks, meeting your smile with a curious one of his own.

You nod, suddenly shy, and stare down at your bracelet. What would he think if he knew how old you were and that he'd been the first to kiss you?

He doesn't ask, but if he does you decide to lie and say you're sixteen. No, fifteen. Then you decide not to offer up any information at all. You don't want to seem young and stupid and you definitely don't want him to know he's got an inexperienced ninth grader on his hands. You pick at a hangnail, wondering if he'll ask you out and if he does, where you can go to show him off to your classmates without revealing your age. Maybe the mall?

"Whoa, you actually live here?" he says after you point out which driveway is yours. "This place is huge."

"Yeah," you say and give a decent, bored shrug. "I've got it all to myself, too. My parents are away." You hold your breath, wondering if he'll take the bait, wondering if you said it right or if you just made a fool out of yourself.

"No kidding," he says, leaning back in his seat and running a finger around the edge of the steering wheel. "Must be great, having a little peace and quiet when you need it. I mean, you've seen how crazy it is over there. Kind of gets to you after a while, especially on Christmas." He glances over at you from beneath sleepy lids and his mouth curves into a hopeful smile. "Want some company?"

"Okay," you croak, and scramble out of the car before you realize he's on his way around to open the door for you. "Oh. Uh, sorry. Uh, this way." Cheeks burning, you scurry up the steps and fumble with the keys. Finally get in, turn off the alarm, and lead him into the family room, praying you haven't left anything embarrassing lying around. "Uh, want a fire?"

"Oh yeah," he says, smiling like you two are sharing a joke, only you don't get it yet. He ditches his coat, wanders over and surveys the contents of your refrigerator, choosing a Molson from your father's stock. "Merry Christmas, beautiful," he says as you set the gas flames dancing merrily along the log. "Jesus, this is great. What a buzz." He chugs the beer, smacks his lips, and retrieves another. Wanders in closer, gives you a lingering once-over, and trails a cool, damp finger down your cheek. "Sweet lady."

"Merry Christmas," you whisper, because the musky heat from his body is hotter than the fireplace and you feel buzzed, too, but not from alcohol. It's almost too much, this miracle of having your dream come true, of being alone with a gorgeous guy who likes you, who thinks you're beautiful and wants to spend the holiday together—

The phone rings.

"Leave it," he says, holding you with his smoky gaze, and when it stops ringing, he takes it off the hook. "No interruptions." He sets his beer on the coffee table, pulls you tight against him, and murmurs, "Now, let's do this right."

You don't answer because suddenly he's kissing you and you haven't even closed your eyes yet. His mouth goes from hungry to ravenous, his chin stubble grates like a loofah, and his tongue forces your jaws so wide the hinges creak.

You wait to be swept away but your arms hang like dead fish around his waist and your tongue is just sort of dodging his. You must be doing it right, though, because he's going crazy all over you like a chained-up dog set free.

He squeezes your breasts. You gasp at the rough pain and your sounds inspire him. He grinds against you, mashing your skin to your bones and chewing on your neck.

"God, you make me so hot," he says and then your shirt goes up and your pants hit the floor. He whips off his own clothes. Together you stumble backward to the couch and fall in a tangled knot. His teeth smack your mouth and his chest is dead weight. You're lying on your hair and are trapped staring at the ceiling.

He tugs your hand down to his thing. You don't know what to do with it, so you do nothing. Impatient, he locks your fingers tight around him and begins moving in your palm.

"Oh yeah, baby," he says.

You drag your head up, freeing your hair, and notice he has dandruff. And that the skin behind his ears is oily. You can smell his scalp.

You shouldn't be able to do that, should you? You shouldn't be able to think while he's kissing you, or care that he's smearing saliva in an ever-widening film around the outside of your mouth. You shouldn't keep whispering, *Wait, stop* in your head or aloud, or wincing when his nails gouge a soft spot or be repelled by his shuddering, sour-beer exhales.

You should be melting, enraptured, adored, moaning and sighing in dreamlike ecstasy—

His hands slide down to tug at your thighs and bruises form beneath his fingers.

You stiffen.

He thrusts against you, prodding for entrance, and then suddenly a red streak shoots up and into you and you zoom away from yourself, but it's too late because you can feel it all, and the invasion is staggering.

"C'mon, don't just lay there," he mutters. "Help me out, will you?"

You turn your face into the cushions because if he puts his sloppy mouth on yours again, you will throw up in it.

He collapses, and you're buried beneath a sweaty landslide. You don't move. Is this it? Did he finish? Are you free?

"Turn over," he gasps, propping himself up and pulling you onto your knees. "This'll do it." He pokes your butt. Your muscles clench in immediate and panicked outrage.

You rip loose and crawl to the corner of the couch. Forget being a ninth grade baby. You've had enough.

He laughs. "Cherry, huh? You'll learn." He fans his groin and stares at his hard-on with almost fatherly pride, then stretches out with his head near your drawn-up legs. "Take a break. I have to cool down."

Your ankle is wet. He's licking your leg. "You mean it's not done?"

"Nope," he says and yawns. "I can go forever when I'm drinking. Hand me my beer, will you, and some of that Johnnie Black over there, too."

You inch away and rise on shaky legs. "I have to go to the bathroom." You skim past the powder room and upstairs to your father's bathroom, locking the door behind you.

The mirror is heartless. You're red, raw, and blotchy. Your hair is knotted, your mouth swollen.

You scald yourself in the shower, scrubbing until his smell fades. Pull on your father's baggiest sweat suit, hoping it's enough to protect you. You wish you'd eaten an onion or drawn a cold sore on your lip. You wish he would leave. Or die. You wish you hadn't told him you were alone in the house.

By the time you creep back to the family room, he's sprawled out snoring. His legs are spread wide and his mouth has gone slack. The bottle of Johnnie Walker is almost half empty.

You turn away, sick.

You take a paring knife from the kitchen and sit on the floor across from him. Push up your sleeve and, hand splayed, lay your forearm across the gleaming marble coffee table. Drag the point across your skin and watch, bemused, as the blood wells and runs in a rivulet down the side of your arm. "One," you say, because he is now your first, the one you will always be damned to remember.

And then his car alarm goes off. He scrambles into his clothes, grabs his keys, and staggers out the front door. You follow him and lock it, listening as the siren is abruptly silenced, as he clomps back up the steps and rattles the knob. Bangs on the door, calls you a bitch and a tease, and chugs off in his car.

Despite the fire, the family room is chilly. You huddle in a chair, but your frayed nerves won't stop trying to flick away his presence.

The knocking starts. It's Ardith, and she won't stop until you let her in. You do, but if you look at her she'll hurt you like her brother just did.

She perches on the coffee table in front of you, moves the paring knife around behind her, and says, "Are you all right?"

"Fine," you mumble, praying she doesn't say another word.

And she doesn't. She goes into the kitchen and makes cappuccino.

You follow her and sit at the table. Look into her eyes and see no malice, only understanding, so you tell her everything.

She hands you a mug and a lit cigarette, then pulls herself up onto the counter and lights one of her own. Watches you with a gaze too old for her age.

"You knew he was a dog," you say, and your voice cracks under the accusation. It isn't fair, but you owe her the right to be right.

"I tried to tell you," she says, shaking her head. "Why do you think I never brought you home with me before?" She sips her coffee. "I don't suppose he wore a condom?"

You blink. "No." You never thought of that. "But I don't think he . . . you know . . . in me."

Ardith shrugs. "Doesn't matter. He doesn't have to. Sperm leaks out and goes on an egg hunt way before that. It's biologically programmed to find and fertilize an egg and the only thing that stops it is death. It's like the Terminator. That's what it does. That's *all* it does."

She's scaring you. You pluck at your bloody sleeve, hating the thought of something happening inside that you have no control over.

"When's your period due?" Ardith says, sliding off the counter.

"This week." It's due December twenty-ninth, and the thirtieth is your fifteenth birthday. Sweet fifteen and never been . . . well, hopefully never been pregnant. You clench a fist and push it into your tender abdomen. Bounce it harder. Imagine dislodging tiny Terminator sperm from your insides and watch the virulent paisleys tumble down into the void. There's no way you can wait four days for this nightmare to end. "How do you bring on a period?"

Ardith doesn't know, so you search online. The morning after pill is perfect, but it needs permission and you'd rather use a hanger on yourself than listen to the fit your parents will pitch if they find out.

"Well, then I hate to say it but you're kind of out of options. The only other idea I can find is major exercise and heat," Ardith says, leaning back in the desk chair and looking at you like she's waiting for you to cry.

You don't. You can't.

So you spend the days until New Year's Eve running up and down the staircase until your muscles burn, sleeping with the heating pad, and dreaming of deserted vineyards.

On New Year's Eve, while you and Ardith are drinking Red Deaths, cursing her brother for giving her a wicked black eye over the rock-on-the-hood incident, and dancing wildly on your marble coffee table, your uterus seizes in a massive cramp, as though it's being dragged down out of you with a dull meat hook. You run to the bathroom to check your underwear and discover the spreading stain, the pale, pink passport to freedom.

You explode back into the family room, where you and Ardith laugh and hug and shriek in celebration. Put on your coats and prance down Main Street, fishing for an exciting way to end the year.

The first taker is an old guy in a Honda, who keeps tugging at his fly.

You say, "Get the hell away from us, you perv," and laugh as he curses you and blasts off. The next is Horace, your housekeeper's son, but he's on his way to a family party and that's not what you had in mind, so you wish him a happy New Year, take the complimentary joints he offers, and keep trolling.

The third car to pull over is Officer Dave Finderne. The joints are hidden safely in your tube top so you descend on him, giddy. "Where have you been? We bought doughnuts and then couldn't find you! We turned fifteen and you missed it! Can we treat you to a cup of coffee? C'mon, you have to say yes; it's a New Year's tradition!"

He shakes his head and smiles, and even though he's turning you down, the sight of him lightens the darkness in the pit of your chest.

"How much have you girls had to drink tonight?" he asks, exiting the car. He's just as tall as you remember and you're glad; you were afraid you had somehow made him bigger than he was.

"Only a little," Ardith says brightly, forgetting to cover her black eye.

"Yeah, just a little," you burble, grinning as he transfers the flashlight's beam from her to you. "For a New Year's Eve toast, you know. Another tradition."

He gives you a look that says you're not fooling anybody and refocuses on Ardith's shiner. "Who did that to you?"

"My jerk brother. He got mad because I . . . um, tweaked his car alarm." She looks at you and you both go off into gales of laughter.

Officer Dave isn't smiling. "That musclehead hit you?"

"Hey, when you're God's gift to women you can do anything you want," you say, wishing you knew how to spit without dribbling. "Ugh. There's a joke."

"You know him, too?" Officer Dave says, looking at you.

"Unfortunately," you say without thinking and grimace as the memory blasts out. You squash it and look away, but not soon enough.

"I can see I'm going to have to have a little talk with this guy," Officer Dave says flatly.

"No, don't," you blurt, exchanging glances with Ardith. Her brother has moved on to a new girl and all but forgotten you two exist. "Please. It's over now and everything's okay. Really. We swear, don't we, Ardith?"

"Yup." She slings an arm around your shoulders, pulls you close, and cups your jaw, squeezing your mouth into a squishy face. "Tell me, Officer; would this face lie?" She laughs and leans against you.

You both stumble back against the patrol car. Officer Dave catches your arm.

"Okay, look, this has got to stop," he says, shaking his head. "I'm not kidding. The safest place for you to be right now is home—"

"Are you aware that most accidents happen in the home?" Ardith says owlishly. "I mean, it would be impossible to slip and fall in the bathtub out here on Main Street, Officer Dave. Have you thought of that?"

"And if we weren't out here then we wouldn't have seen you again, and that would have been awful." Your face crumples, thinking about how awful it would have been. "You never visit us, Officer Dave. We miss you. We like you. Don't you like us?"

"Okay, that corks it," he says, opening the back of the patrol car and escorting you both inside. "Seems like I'm making a habit of taking you home." He slides into the driver's seat and sits a minute.

"You know, you're decent kids and I don't mind cutting you a break, but maybe I'm not doing the right thing. Maybe I *should* be transporting you to a clinic or a youth shelter instead. I don't think you belong there, but I could be wrong." He meets your gaze in the rearview mirror. "What do you think?"

"I think," you say carefully, making sure each word is whole and perfectly formed so he'll know you're sincere, "we should go to my house and stay there. And you could stay, too, and we could give you coffee. Or," you frown, trying to remember what Lourdes left in the fridge, "we could give you a sandwich. We don't have any doughnuts and nobody made cookies. I'm sorry." You lean forward, hooking your fingers through the wire mesh dividing the front from the back. The smells are better here; crisp cologne mixed with leather mixed with shotgun. "We could bring it all out to the car and have a little party. We could talk. It'll be fun."

He removes his baseball cap and runs his hand through his hair. "That's a very nice offer, but I can't accept." He sighs. "I'll take you both home."

"I'm sleeping at Blair's," Ardith says, tugging down her skirt. "If I was home, I'd have to spend the night locked in my room."

Officer Dave mutters something under his breath and pulls the squad car away from the curb. "Don't you girls have any other family you can stay with?"

"My only grandmother is in a nursing home in California," Ardith says.

You think of your unhappy, housebound grandmother and your incontinent grandfather. "No, but you could always take us home to your wife and say you found us in baskets on the doorstep. We'd be good, wouldn't we, Ardith?"

"We'd be sterling," she says. "We don't eat a lot, either. Blair has a debit card so we could even pay our own way. C'mon, Officer Dave, adopt us."

"I don't think you'd want an old stick in the mud like me for a father," he says, turning onto your street and cruising slowly past the lifeless houses.

Ardith stares down at her lap and doesn't answer.

You gaze out the window, wondering if he'll remember which mausoleum is yours, and are pleased when he pulls straight into your driveway.

He gets out and opens your door. "Now, do you promise to stay put tonight? If I catch you like this again, I'm going to have to call family services . . ."

"We'll stay put," Ardith says, subdued.

"We're not really bad, you know," you say.

"No, I know you're not," he says, all signs of laughter gone. He shifts and rests his wide, steady hands on his gun belt. "Look, let me give you a piece of advice. Don't put yourself out on the streets at night. If you want to wander around town, do it in the daytime, and don't ever do it drunk. One wrong choice, one time, and it's too late." He smoothes his mustache and watches you both with serious eyes. "You're good kids, and I really don't want to be the one to find your bodies lying in the weeds on the side of the road, okay? So relax, will you? Don't be in such a hurry to grow up."

"We won't," you say, peeking up at him from beneath your hair. "Are you mad at us?"

"No." He clears his throat. "Let's just say I've gotten used to seeing your smiling mugs and I want to keep it that way." He holds out his hand. "So are we square?"

Happiness blooms and you seize his hand. "Square."

"You guys need me, you call. I'll be watching out for you." He shakes Ardith's hand, too, and trains his spotlight on your front door until you wave an "all clear."

The night goes flat. New Year's Eve. Big deal. You wander back to the mess in the family room, toss the joints on the bar, and plunk down on the couch.

"He always shows up when we're being stupid," Ardith says, curling up on the opposite end of the couch. "Maybe he's like our guardian angel or something."

"Maybe." You'd like to believe, but it's hard when your thighs are covered in fading, finger-shaped bruises and Ardith's wearing a black eye.

You surf until you find a televised New Year's Eve celebration, but it's so boring you both fall asleep before the clock strikes midnight.

When you wake up, you have your feet jammed against Ardith's butt for warmth and your mother is standing over you, fresh from the cold and looking mad as hell.

Before Ardith takes over, I want to make sure my parents' choices are clearly credited and defined, not rewritten or whitewashed with lawyerspeak.

Oh, do I sound bitter? Funny. What would I have to be bitter about?

No, I don't want any more water. Thanks. I just want to get this over with.

So I woke up on New Year's Day with horrible cramps and before I could even pull the room into focus, I saw my mother looming over me, her furious face perched on top of a fat, hairy dog's body.

She pointed a human hand and snapped, "What is this?"

The bar was littered with open liquor bottles, an empty orange juice container, a silver cocktail shaker, brimming ashtray, and two joints.

My mother yanked off her new coyote coat and tossed it over the armchair.

The fur was thick and gleaming. Tipped with beige and gold.

I couldn't stop staring at it.

"I can't believe what I'm seeing." She glanced at Ardith, who was awake but pretending not to be, then back at me. "Where did you get those slutty clothes?"

I tugged at the sparkly, black tube top and matching tube skirt. Nudged the satin platforms farther under the couch. Ardith was wearing the same outfit, only in red. "I bought them." My voice was hoarse from sleep.

"I see." She picked up a joint, examined it, and looked at me. "So you had a party last night. Brilliant. Make me liable for every minor in town. Who else was here?"

"Nobody." I was shivering. Cramping.

She laughed without humor. "Right. Let me remind you of what I do for a living, Blair. I represent the defendant. The one accused of screwing up. To successfully do that, I have to out-think everyone; my client, the prosecution, the jury, everyone. I've made men cry on the stand and veteran cops turn on each other." She perched on the edge of the coffee table. "I'm not the one you want to lie to, little girl."

I couldn't look away.

"Nobody else was here, Mrs. Brost," Ardith said, sitting up and smoothing her outfit. Her voice was strained. "It was just us."

My mother ignored her. "Why would you do this, Blair?" she said, pulling one of my platforms out from under the couch. Her eyebrows rose at the sight of the scuffed, worn sole. "Especially now, when you know how important it is for us to remain above reproach." She tossed the shoe on the floor and stood up. "Well?"

I glanced at Ardith.

My mother swooped down, gripped my chin between her fingers, and turned my face to hers. "Don't look over there. Look over here. Why did you do this?"

I twisted away. My heart was pounding and my abdomen cramping. "I'm sorry, okay? It was no big deal. Nothing happened."

"Wrong." My mother was as lethal as lightning. "Something *has* happened, and it's not going to happen again." She glared at Ardith. "Are you local?"

"Um . . . yes," Ardith said, drawing back into the couch and staring up at her.

"Good," my mother said. "Get your things and go home. My daughter does not need your negative influence and you won't be welcome here again."

"Mom, no." My period was punishing me. "Don't blame her."

"I'm not going to pursue this matter any further," my mother continued, displaying the joints. "But if I find out you've been around here—and rest assured, I *will* find out—then I'm going to initiate legal action."

"It's not her fault," I ground out, doubled over with cramps.

"Do you understand what I mean by 'legal action'?" she said, never taking her eyes off Ardith's pasty face. "Do you understand that I can tie your family up in court for years? Do you know how expensive that will be?"

"Don't," I yodeled as she escorted an unresisting Ardith out through the front door and closed it firmly behind her.

Chapter 10

Ardith

Blair's mother caused some really bad heartache and while I'd like to say it's over now and I don't hold a grudge, I'd be lying. Mrs. Brost can rot in hell for all I care. Now I understand why Blair was so hung up on the "intent" aspect of Wendy's death.

Because her mother screwed me, too.

Just like she intended.

Chapter 11

Ardith's Story

The frigid air slaps you awake. You stand on the front steps and look blankly around the cul-de-sac. Nothing stirs. Is it early? Probably. Who knows? The only absolute is that your bladder is full and clamoring for release.

You press your legs together, wanting to hold yourself like a little kid. You'll never even make it to the end of the block.

But you can't go back in there. You can't. Oh God, you have to.

You knock. Mrs. Brost answers and you mumble your request.

She hesitates and you inch forward, knowing the only way you're going to make it now is with a running start.

"No," Mrs. Brost says and closes the door in your face.

"But I have to go," you say stupidly to the closed door and then, as if to reinforce your statement, pee seeps into your panty hose.

Shock flings you down the steps, around the side of the house and behind a dwarf, spike-leafed holly bush. You yank at your clothes, squat and hide your face as steam rises around you.

Few people see you trudging the length of Main Street in splattered, red satin platforms and a creased, glittering mini. Of those who do, several honk and shout offers. You wrap your arms around your waist, making yourself a smaller target.

Clop. Clop. Clop. Your thighs are chapped and raw, your face burning and your head throbbing. Happy New Year. One minute you're sleeping, lost in dreams, and the next Blair's mother is staring down at you like you're dog crap stinking up her lawn.

You're a bad influence. Stay away from my daughter.

You punch a mailbox as you pass and wince as the tremors penetrate your benumbed knuckles. Stupid move. No point in getting excited. Mrs. Brost will bitch today and be gone again by tomorrow. She has no reason to stick around.

Nothing's going to change.

You creep into your house. Nobody's awake yet so you shower, change into sweats, brush your teeth, and make coffee. Have a cigarette right at the table, blowing smoke rings to the rhythm of the ratcheting snores echoing in from the bodies cluttering the TV room.

You think about calling Blair, but don't. Why give her mother another chance to humiliate you? This is worse than being condemned because of your last name. This is personal and the force of the injustice makes you boil.

You're not bad. You would never hurt Blair. And Officer Dave likes you, even though he knows about your family. Mrs. Brost doesn't even know your name.

You haul the ham out of the fridge, jab it full of cloves, and put it in the oven to bake. Whip up a big batch of blueberry pancakes and set the bowl aside until you feel like ending your solitude and luring in the masses. Set out plates, silverware, butter, syrup, and powdered sugar.

There. You've done everything right.

You kick back with another cigarette and when Phone Dent wanders in from the TV room, scratching his stomach and yawning, you even manage a civil greeting. "Morning. Coffee's on, if you want some."

"Good deal," he says, giving you an odd look before pouring a cup. His hair is whorled, his jeans sag on his skinny hips, and a carpet pattern mottles his cheek. "You missed one helluva party," he says, rubbing his bleary eyes and sipping his coffee. His face lights up and he lifts the cup in tribute. "Good stuff. Better 'n Connie's."

"Thanks," you say, because it's not often a compliment heads your way. "There are blueberry pancakes for breakfast later, too." You stop, wondering why you're telling him this. Why you're talking to him at all. He's a jerk, a pig, and a user, just like the rest of them. Just like what you're never going to be.

"Oh yeah," he says, and his mouth creaks into a sleepy grin. "I'm there. Call me when they're ready." He winks and slouches back into the TV room.

You watch him go, bitter heat spreading through your veins. You jab out your cigarette, drain your mug, and spoon batter into the frying pan. Cook three whopper pancakes and slap them onto a plate. You're in the midst of drowning the butter-smeared tops in syrup when Phone Dent wanders back in.

"Smells good," he says, leaning against the counter next to you.

"Tastes better," you say, stuffing a forkful into your mouth and chewing. "Yum. Have at it." You pick up your plate and mug.

"What? Hey, I thought you were making them," he says, frowning.

"Nope." You point to the batter bowl. "All the pancakes in the world are right there waiting for you. Enjoy." You stroll to your room, a deafening silence in your wake and a small triumph under your belt. You finish your breakfast while reading a podiatry book and thinking about what will happen come tomorrow. Mrs. Brost should be gone again by then. You'll see Blair at school and laugh at how stupid people are to think they can keep you apart.

Only when you get to school her mother's black Mercedes is hogging two spaces in the courtyard parking lot and Blair gazes out at you from behind the tinted glass. Her mother lowers her sunglasses and gives you a steady look over the rims.

You stumble and keep walking, past the car, up the steps, and into the vestibule. Down the hall to an empty classroom, where you watch the bustling courtyard from the corner of the window until the bell rings and Blair stalks through the crowd into the school.

You run to meet her, scanning the surge of oncoming traffic, but can't find her. Some clod steps on your flopping shoelace and nearly gives you whiplash. You crouch, disappearing into a sea of scissoring legs to retie your shoe.

Gary, the BK Romeo, stops in front of you and, grinning, says, "Hey Ardith, while you're down there . . ."

"Go to hell," you say, brushing him off.

"Save me a seat between you and your lezzie girlfriend," he says, smirking.

You shoot up from the floor. "What's that supposed to mean?"

"Like you don't know," he drawls, facing you as he ambles away.

"Sounds more like *you* don't know," you say, holding on to your shaky, *lirgas* attitude with everything you've got. Of all the people who could've repeated ninth grade, why did it have to be him?

"New Year's Eve?" he says in a loud, taunting voice that earns more than a few curious glances. "You and your girlfriend down on Main Street, getting picked up by the cops?" He cocks his head and grins. "I saw you guys hanging all over each other." He squeezes his mouth into a kissy face. "Look familiar?"

"You don't know what you're talking about," you say, but it sounds lame even to you.

"Hey, I saw what I saw," he says, shrugging and burying his hands in his pants pockets. "If you don't believe me, ask Marvin. He was there, too."

"Where?" you ask, knowing you shouldn't.

"The pool hall right across the street," he says. "What, do you think you and your girlfriend are the only people out on New Year's Eve?"

Your brain is scrambling to deflect this ambush, but it's crippled by the unexpected shock. Of all the people who had to see you with your arm around Blair. . . . You struggle for a worthy defense but the bell rings.

Gary turns and, whistling, fades into the crowd.

You smooth the tension from your face and bolt into homeroom. Slide into your seat. Notice the odd bubble of silence surrounding you and the whispers threading along the fringes of the room. You look up and around. Stares slip away before you can catch them like a dozen biting horseflies.

Gary's gossip couldn't have gotten this far already.

So you double-check, but your bra straps aren't showing and your pants are zipped. You look up and immediately connect with Kimmer Ashton, Jeremy's girlfriend, who's perched on the windowsill, swinging her legs and watching you. She holds your gaze for a heartbeat, then blinks, slow and deliberate, and looks away.

You do, too, but it's too late to pretend you don't see her mocking smile. It tells you plenty, like she knows it will, but it doesn't tell you why, and she knows that, too.

So you stifle your fear, shrug like you don't care, and get busy writing your name in your notebook. Homeroom ends in seven minutes and if you drag it out, you can make your preoccupation with penmanship last just about that long. You stare at the page. Your name is a lone bottle floating on an ocean of blue-lined paper. You frown and erase the small, cramped letters. The words disappear but the impression remains and there's nothing you can do about that.

The bell finally rings and you bolt down to Blair's locker. This'll be your first time late to class all year and you'd rather not ruin a perfect record, but you need to know what happened yesterday and what will happen from now on. And you need to tell her about Gary and Kimmer.

You meet her halfway.

"Walk me to class, Ardith, I can't be late," she says grimly.

"So what happened?" you ask, hustling to keep up with her angry strides. She's cutting a swath down the center of the crowd with all the finesse of a logger's chain saw.

"I'm not allowed to hang around with you anymore," she says, arriving at her classroom and swinging around to look at you. "If I do, my parents are either going to send me to live with my grandmother—and that's three hours away—or to boarding school." She tosses her head, but her hair is trapped in an elastic and the ponytail has no attitude; it only flops once and lays still. "Isn't that great?"

"What? But they don't even know me," you say, panicking. "Not even my name!"

"They don't care. It has nothing to do with you and everything to do with them," she says, glancing into the room. "I have to go. For real." She snorts and gestures to her red sweater and black khakis. "Like my lame outfit? My mother is now supervising my wardrobe because I wasn't living up to my pristine Brost image. Right."

You watch as she reaches into the neck of her sweater and pulls out a silver locket on a chain. You don't have to lean close to read the inscription because you were the one who told the jeweler what to write, waiting calmly as the line of impatient Christmas shoppers grew long and cranky behind you.

The front says, *Wendy D 4ever,* and on the back, *2 B luv A.*

It's the first time you've seen her wear it.

A cold hand closes around your heart.

"First Wendy, now you," she says, and walks into class without a backward look.

"You're going to be late to class, Ardith," says a passing teacher.

No you're not, because you need your perfect record now more than ever, so you take off with the echo of "No running in the hallway!" pounding in your ears. You make it to honors English before the teacher arrives and take your seat, middle row, last desk.

Gary's friend Marvin's in front of you, Kimmer smack in the center of the room.

You whip open your notebook and find the page where you'd written your name. The impression remains. You still exist.

"Hey Ardith, I hear you had a hot time on New Year's Eve," Kimmer sings out, giving you an arch look. She's perched on her desk with her feet on the chair, an Abercrombie vulture with perfect teeth and a sixth grade nose job.

An icicle screws into your stomach. Kimmer doesn't talk to you and you don't talk to her. *Ever.* But she doesn't talk to Gary or

Marvin, either—you all inhabit low rungs on the loser ladder—so this time she must have made an exception.

The air thins as the class sucks in a collective, anticipatory breath.

"Kind of a lez-be-friends thing, right?" She smiles and her incisors are pointy.

"You're a fucking asshole," you say and your voice wobbles at the end, right as the teacher walks in. Luckily he's calling for order and misses your words and the gasps of horrified delight. You turn away, tamp down your rising panic, but the room is too hot and the teacher blurs into the chalkboard.

You've done it now, publicly told off Kimmer, a superior power, which means she has to destroy you. The New Year's Eve rumor will be all over school soon and Gary will claim he knew you guys were gay ever since he saw you in the dark field after the swim club dance. And it won't matter that everyone always thought Gary was a jerk because the gossip is juicy enough to make up for it.

A balled-up note lands on your desk.

You stare down at it. Your heart is a hummingbird. The note could say anything. It could say, "Don't listen to them." It could say, "Die, lezzie slut."

Another one arrives. The teacher is writing on the board and misses the second, third, and fourth notes that rain down around you.

Emboldened, Marvin swivels in his seat and lays a full sheet of paper on your desk. He glances around the room, basking in the pack's long-denied approval, and waits eagerly for your reaction.

You gaze down at the crudely drawn picture of two naked, humping girls and your fingers roll up tight.

"Lesbo," Marvin whispers.

"Good one," someone says, snickering under his breath.

Marvin quivers with pleasure at being acknowledged. "Hootchie lezzie." His lips move and his fingers twitch as he hunts for one more name.

The one that will get him hurt.

"Don't," you say flatly.

He rears back, startled and momentarily cowed, then rallies and delivers the final blow: "I don't have to listen to you. *Bull dyke.*"

It's inevitable, you guess, that the teacher hears and turns back to the class right as your fist completes its roundhouse swing and bounces off Marvin's face. He's seen it coming, though, and ducks, so instead of breaking his nose, your knuckles connect with his bony, unyielding forehead, and the crunch that stuns the room is from you.

"Hey! What the heck did I just see?" the teacher yells, striding down the aisle toward you. "Ardith! Marvin!"

"My head," Marvin moans, crumpling. "She punched me in my head!" He gropes his face and searches his hands. No blood, just a fast-rising knot.

"Oh God," you whisper, closing your eyes as pain sweeps your body. Something inside you is broken. Everything inside you is broken.

The teacher hustles you and Marvin to the nurse's office. The nurse checks head and hand, decides neither of you has done irreparable damage, and dispenses ice packs with cool, practiced efficiency.

"You're gonna get in trouble, you know," Marvin says while the nurse calls down to the assistant principal's office. He touches the goose egg and winces. "I have witnesses. The whole class saw you do it."

"The whole class thinks you're a loser," you say dully. If you'd broken his nose he wouldn't be talking right now, and if you'd broken your hand you'd be on your way to the hospital instead of sitting here waiting for the ax to fall. "They hate you more than they hate me. Christ, get a clue." You grit your teeth and turn away from his wounded gaze. "You really think that if you make a big deal out of this you're gonna be some kind of hero?" Snorting, you give the knife one last twist. Why not? You have no reason to be good anymore. No one wants a lezzie slut for a friend, or for a podiatrist. "Well, you're not. You're going to be the same old loser, except now, because of your big mouth, you're going to be 'Marvin who got his ass kicked by a girl.' Is that what you want? You want to be an even bigger laughingstock?" You shrug. "Fine, then go ahead and make a big deal out of it."

"That's not what'll happen," he mutters, scowling at the floor.

"Wanna bet?" you say, right as the assistant principal strides through the door with Mr. Everett, your guidance counselor, hot on his heels.

Under direct questioning, Marvin sulkily admits he called you names but says he doesn't remember what he called you or who else was involved.

"You *do* know, because your teacher has already told me what both you and the notes said," Mr. Everett says quietly.

"Well, if you already know, then what're you asking me for?" Marvin says.

"Don't make it worse," you say under your breath.

Marvin sneaks you a glance. "Okay, so yeah. I did."

"Why?"

Another shrug. He's offered up all he's going to.

"This incident will be added to your permanent records, of

course," the assistant principal says, sighing and running a hand over his bald spot. "Marvin, I'm signing you up for a diversity tolerance workshop with a peer counselor tomorrow after school." And in the next breath, "Ardith, you know our zero-tolerance rule about fighting. I'm afraid you've earned a day's suspension."

The room tilts and you clutch the edge of the desk.

Not a suspension. You've kept your permanent record spotless. No failing grades, no detention. Few absences, no fights. Not even one gentle, chiding "Is not working up to capacity" or "Needs to try harder," because you've always had to try harder just to reach your capacity.

"He gets a workshop and I get suspended?" you choke out. "But he started it! I was just minding my own business . . ." Panic steals your breath. "It's not fair."

"Sticks and stones, Ardith," the assistant says, not unkindly. "Life isn't fair. There will always be people who say things you don't like, but that does not give you the right to physically assault them. Do you understand?"

You struggle for a moment to dislodge the sordid details that will explain why it wasn't your fault, and why you don't deserve to be suspended, but they won't shake loose. You've been private too long. You bow your head, your neck creaking under the weight.

"Do you understand, Ardith?" he repeats.

You nod. Yeah, sure, you understand. You understand that people like Kimmer and Mrs. Brost and even Marvin will always be granted license to destroy simply because they use the adult-sanctioned weapon of words.

"Look, let's not be hasty on this suspension," Mr. Everett says. "Ardith's never been in trouble before and I'm not sure we'd be accomplishing anything by—"

"She punched this boy in the head," the assistant says. "And zero-tolerance means just that. What kind of message would we be sending to the other students and their parents if we didn't enforce our own rules?"

"But he admitted that he instigated it," Mr. Everett says doggedly. "There were extenuating circumstances."

You glance at him, then down at his feet. His shoes are wide and worn thin on the outsides. He must walk like a gorilla.

"Look, don't make it into a big deal, okay?" Marvin says, hunching low when they turn to look at him. "It's over. I don't want her suspended."

"Well, you should have thought of that sooner, Marvin," the assistant says. "What's done can't be undone, and someone has to pay the piper. Now, take your ice pack and go back to class. Ardith, you'll finish out the day in Mr. Everett's office and tomorrow you'll serve your suspension. And I don't want to see either one of you back here for fighting again." He nods at Mr. Everett and the nurse and walks out.

Marvin goes back to class.

You follow Mr. Everett to Guidance. He *does* walk like a gorilla, rolling along on bowed legs and crushing the outside edges of his squeegy, rubber-soled shoes.

You spend half the morning tucked into the corner of his office, doing your homework assignments as they come in, your gaze locked onto your notebook, your ears ringing with humiliation. You mumble thanks when Mr. Everett brings you a cup of hot cocoa from the cafeteria, but you can't bring yourself to look at him. He calls your house to tell your mother about the suspension but the line is busy and he can't get through. You don't tell him it's because she's designing an adult website. You don't tell him anything at all.

Something flutters at the edge of your vision. Blair is standing out in the hallway, peering in through the window and waving frantically. She mouths something, points, and ducks out of sight.

You look at Mr. Everett. "Can I go to the bathroom, please?"

"Sure, but come right back," he says, smiling as if he's glad you've decided he's not such an ogre after all.

"Thanks," you say and hurry out.

The halls are dead—classes are still in session—and you jog to the bathroom, where Blair is yanking a brush through her hair and scowling into the mirror.

"Oh my God, Ardith, I heard," she says, whirling as you walk in. She scrapes the hair from her brush and tosses the knot toward the garbage can. It falls short and drifts to the floor. "Are you all right? I can't believe it." She catches your cautioning look and shakes her head. "It's okay, there's nobody here. I already checked. So what the hell happened?"

Your stomach spasms. You feel bloated and obscene. "Gary saw us with Officer Dave on New Year's Eve. He saw when I put my arm around you and made that squishy face. He's telling everybody we're gay." You can't meet her gaze in the mirror. The swim dance memory has always been a warm, deep pocket of water in an otherwise shallow, chilly pool but here, now, and under these circumstances, it seems more like a sinkhole than a sanctuary. "Kimmer's passing it on."

"Kimmer?" Blair's voice squeaks. "That little bitch!" Her hand whips the locket back and forth on its chain. "Oh God, I swear, I'm gonna kill her."

"You can't, you'll get in trouble," you say. The hairball drifts across the tile and clings to your shoe. "You can't even *say* you're going to kill her, remember? The school has a zero-tolerance policy for making 'terrorist' threats, too."

"Oh, but she and Gary can go around spreading rumors and nothing happens to them?" Blair demands, planting her hands on her hips. "What's that about?"

" 'Life isn't fair.' " You mimic the assistant principal, but you're too miserable to be angry. "I'm suspended tomorrow for fighting. It's going on my permanent record." The room blurs. "Everything's ruined."

"Oh, for . . . I can't believe this," Blair says, scrubbing her hand across her forehead, and in that moment, with her set jaw and fierce gaze, she looks more Brost then Blair. "What the hell are we doing wrong?" She paces the room.

You slump against the cool, painted cinder-block wall and whack your head on the corner of the paper towel dispenser but the pain barely registers. You must have winced, though, because Blair snakes a hand up behind you and rubs the back of your skull.

"You have this weird, tangled cowlick going on back here, Ardith." Scowling, she pulls out her brush. "Stand still."

You can feel the brush working through the knot, patiently separating the strands, parting it into sections, working and smoothing it all back together.

"There. That's better." She nods, satisfied, and wedges her brush into her pocket.

"Thanks," you say, mourning the loss of the warmth at your neck and wishing the knot had been bigger. Wishing it had encompassed your whole stupid head. "Blair?" You meet her unwavering gaze in the mirror. "What're we going to do?"

"I don't know," she says, sighing and rubbing the side of her face. "It's too late for *lirgas.* Gary's stupid babbling might have been ignored—nobody ever listens to him anyway—but now that Kimmer stuck her big fat face into it . . ." She stops, cocks her head, and her gaze brightens. "Hey, you don't think she's pushing this rumor because she's afraid Jeremy still likes you, do you?"

"No," you say immediately, because the thought is absurd.

"Think about it," Blair says, pacing again. "She wants to see you crawl, Ardith. Why? What's her motivation here?"

"She gets off on it," you say. "It's something to do, like a sport."

"I don't know about that," Blair says, shaking her head. "People don't usually go out of their way to crush other people unless they really hate them, or there's something in it for them . . ." She stops and pins you with a piercing, sparkling gaze. "You want to pay Kimmer back and kill the gay rumor at the same time? Be with Jeremy."

"What?"

"Go be with him. Kiss him. Grope him. Make him cheat on Kimmer with you." She laughs and her rising excitement buffets you like a sweeping Santa Ana wind. "Come on, it's a great idea and she can't do shit about it because there's no school rule about messing around with somebody else's boyfriend! Oh my God, I'm a genius."

"I can't kiss Jeremy," you say stupidly.

"Why not? You wanted to last Thanksgiving," she says.

Yes you did, but you don't anymore and you stammer as much.

"So what? You don't have to like him to kiss him," Blair says with an impatient look. "All you have to do is endure it. Trust me on this, Ardith, because I know."

She means your brother. Thanks to him, her experience now exceeds yours, but you still have your own grim memories of shadowy hallways pressing against your back and the tinny taste of blood and foreign saliva flooding your mouth. The only kiss you've ever given willingly was the one shared with Blair and even that carries its own dark, confusing legacy.

"I can't," you say, miserable. You've walked the balance beam between home and school so carefully, and for so long, that falling off immobilized you. No step is a safe one, so it's safer to take none at all.

She gazes back at you for a considered moment and you get the feeling that she sees more than you've ever shown her. You can't break the connection, can't shut her out because she's too far in and you're terrified that she'll guess what you've only wondered at yourself, and hate you for it.

"Well, I can," she says finally and the air crackles. Her locket catches the glare from the overhead fluorescents and flashes silver lightning. She yanks her sweater up over her head, revealing the sheer, tight, black mesh T-shirt underneath. Ties the sweater around her waist and bends over, fluffing up her hair. Straightens. "There. That ought to do it." Her bra is the same black lace one she wore on Christmas Day. "I'll meet you for lunch, okay?"

"I can't, I'm stuck in Guidance." She's so cold and distant that she's scaring you. "Blair? What if he doesn't do anything? I mean, what if he blows you off?"

"Then I'll be a laughingstock," she says shortly, pinching her cheeks until they glow. "Oh, excuse me. A *lezzie-ho* laughingstock and Kimmer will win again and we will lose again and Gary's yap will go right on flapping because nobody's humiliated but us, and we don't count. Okay?"

Her bluntness is a rude shove and you fall back a step. Somehow you've shrunken or Blair has grown because she towers over you now, and you used to be the same height. "Are you mad at me?"

Blair's eyes flicker and a thin smile curves her lips. "No. I'm mad *for* you." She strides out.

The room throbs with residual energy. You meet your gaze in the mirror and see she's right. You have no righteous anger, only despair. And fear. You look like a victim. You pee and walk back to Guidance.

"You've been gone a long time," Mr. Everett says, glancing at his watch.

"I had a problem in the bathroom," you mumble, avoiding his gaze. He'll think you mean your period, which is what you want because then he'll get all weird and drop the subject. You've heard your brother's girlfriends say this is so a thousand times.

"Oh," he says and turns away, scrabbling around for something on his desk. "Well, uh, your history homework is here now, so you might as well start it."

"Sure," you say and open the book, but you don't do much reading because you're thinking of Blair. You don't know whether to curse her recklessness or applaud the brazen, irreversible payback she's about to unload on Kimmer.

And you worry about the backlash. Because there *will* be one.

There always is.

I feel bad about punching Marvin. I mean, yeah, maybe he deserved it, but they all did, so why did I take it out on him? Why punish the kid who's been a public punching bag his whole life? I mean, even his *friends* pound on him.

I never thought I was the kind of person who'd kick a dog when it was down, but I went and did it anyway.

And I know why, too. Because I could. Because he was the safest one, the kid with no power or high-status friends to come back at me.

So I sunk as low as every other bully and that makes me sick.

You know these kids around the country who can't take the pressure? Who lose it and go ballistic? Well, I'm telling you this is how it starts. Taunting. Teasing. Tormenting.

Torture someone enough and the pain turns to anger.

The only thing worse than being invisible is being visible and powerless.

I shouldn't have hit Marvin. I should have hit Gary or Kimmer, but Gary would have hit me back, and I wasn't brave enough to scale those clique walls to get up to Kimmer.

Blair was, though. She not only scaled them, she *picnicked* on them.

When she got mad, all of that potency inside her just blossomed, like she'd waited her whole life for that first, sweet victory.

Stop her? No way. I couldn't.

Because it brought something out in me, too, and I'd be lying if I said I didn't like it.

Chapter 12

Blair

So now you see why I had to do something about the rumor. I mean, when Ardith walked into that bathroom she looked ready to kill herself. Terrified and totally beaten. That freaked me out because she's the strong one, and if this was bad enough to take her down, then it had to be serious.

The gay rumor thing hit her harder than it hit me. Of course, at that point I didn't really understand that keeping her record and her reputation clean meant more to her than just smoothing a path toward med school.

I didn't understand that keeping clean was her way of building a life.

I was more upset at my mother. Who the hell was she to pick my friends? I mean, being in a world without Wendy sucks; I absolutely refuse to be in one without Ardith, too. That's just not an option.

So I was already pretty wired when Ardith told me about

Kimmer pushing that rumor and there was no way that little bitch was going to get away with it. She'd hurt Ardith on purpose and now she was going to get hurt, too.

The only thing is, I didn't realize how totally dedicated I was to getting even.

I just didn't know.

No, I'm not trying to justify my actions, but I'll tell you this: It felt damn good to give out, instead of receive. To act, instead of being acted upon.

What, you think that sounds spiteful? All right, then think of it like this: Sooner or later, the current inning ends and even the catcher gets a turn at bat. And if he's been roughed up and knocked down enough, then there's a real good chance he's going to deck the other team's pitcher with a line drive of his own.

It's called provoking a reaction. Except the instigator never really knows exactly how the victim's going to react, does he? But that's the chance he takes when he instigates. That *maybe* things won't turn out the way he's planned. That *maybe* his victim's got a hammer in his pocket and only needs to be pushed one more stupid inch before—

No, no, no, I didn't crown Kimmer with a hammer. I didn't even touch her.

But I got her good. She paid, and she learned.

Ardith says I paid, too, but I don't mind. It was worth it.

Oh, was I smiling? Well, it wasn't *all* bad. In fact, some of it was a total blast.

Make no mistake: what we did to get here, we did together.

What? Where did I learn so much about baseball?

From my father, back when we were still a family, and all on the same team.

Do I love my parents?

Next question.

No, better than that, rewind to New Year's Day.

Chapter 13

Blair's Story

Ardith's kicked out and you're in the bathroom, peeling off your bloody, black panty hose, while your mother waits in your bedroom. You hate her being alone in there with your stuff, so you change your tampon and put on a velour bathrobe. Throw your clothes in the hamper and pad down the hall to your room, pausing in the doorway.

Your mother is pulling the last pushpin from the "Rainbow Bridge" poem and removing the sheet of paper from the wall.

It's out of her hands and into yours before either of you knows how it happened.

"I bought you a frame for that," she says, watching as you skirt the bed and place the poem out of her reach on the desk.

"I like it the way it is," you say, smoothing the paper's edges.

Frowning, she traces the faint, pure white square that remains on the wall where the page used to hang. "I can't believe the paint in here has darkened already. Is it this bad in the rest of the house, too, or only where you're smoking?"

You open your mouth to deny the accusation, but shut it. Smoking is the lightweight violation, the lead-in to the list of punishable offenses, and you have a feeling you'd better save your best for what comes later.

"I'm glad you didn't lie to me just now," she says, perching on the edge of your bed and patting the spot beside her. "Come and sit down. We have to talk."

You're wise to her action. Change of venue, change of tactics. You pull out the desk chair and sink into it. "I can hear you fine from here."

Her mouth tightens. "All right," she says, nodding. "You're angry at me for embarrassing you in front of that girl. I can understand that."

You shrug. She's wrong, but you let it slide because anything you say can and will be used against you.

"But you have to understand something, too," she says in a voice that's soft in the middle but hardening at the edges like old cheese. "We trusted you to act in a mature, responsible manner and you betrayed that trust. You risked not only *your*, but *our* entire future by bringing illegal drugs into the house. God only knows what could have happened." She frowns but she isn't really seeing *you*, she's seeing a potential monkey wrench tossed into the works. Somehow you've become the melanoma waging sneaky, silent mutiny while she attends to the more important business of becoming a Your Honor.

"Don't worry, it won't happen again," you say, just to end the whole thing.

"Oh, I know it won't," she says, picking up Wendy's urn. The lamplight catches the prism-cut glass and shoots sharp, golden diamonds across her face. "Your father and I were wrong to allow you so much unsupervised time. We see that now." She places the urn on the nightstand and shakes her head, as if unable to understand affording the past such a prominent and unavoidable position in the present. "We're grounding you to all outside activities until you've reearned our trust."

"Fine," you say, folding the bathrobe cuffs to your wrists. No higher, though, or the knife notch in your arm will become visible. It's healing nicely, thanks to Ardith's aloe vera gel, but you've both examined the wound and are in perfect agreement: you'll carry the scar.

"Fine," she says, rising. "Now get dressed. A water pipe broke on the Vineyard so the Lunas have been kind enough to invite us all to an open house at their home instead."

"I thought I was grounded," you say, picking at your sleeve.

"Behave and get dressed," your mother says evenly. "Camella Luna says Dellasandra is eager to see you again. I told her you felt the same way."

Liar, you think, and when she leaves, you lock the door behind her. Kneel and root around in the folds of the old, plaid blanket still gracing the orthopedic mattress planted near your bed. It's become a shrine of sorts, similar to the crosses you've seen staked out along highways or tacked to ravaged trees. You haul out a velvet box. The locket is from Ardith and holds a snip of Wendy's fur. You fasten it around your neck and get dressed.

Your mother lets your father drive her Mercedes to the Lunas. The house is historic, the massive, fieldstone front completely covered in ivy. Squared-off hedges line the walk and ancient trees tower over the expansive lawn.

"Camella says this used to be a hundred-acre estate but it was divided up and sold off during the Depression," your mother says. "Impressive."

"You know what I see when I look at this place?" your father says, ambling around the car and joining your mother on the brick walk. "Sky-high maintenance bills. Give me a new house any day of the week."

"Cooperate, and you'll soon have one," your mother says and starts, as if suddenly remembering your existence. She and your father exchange looks.

A surge of hate washes in and pools in your chest.

Dellasandra, stunning in scarlet cashmere, answers the door.

"Happy New Year, dear," your mother says, smiling and stepping into the fragrant, decorated foyer. "It's so nice to see you again. You look lovely. Is that the new Betsey Johnson dress your mother was telling me about?"

"Mm-hmm, thanks. My parents are in the main drawing room right through there," Della says, reaching past your startled father and locking onto your arm. "Hi, Blair. What took you so long? Come with me to get a cranberry juice."

Your mother's schmoozing dies on her lips.

Dellasandra leads you off and the sleek, glittering crowd casts fond glances as she passes. A politician even *you* recognize calls, "Come on over here, Della, and give your old pal a hug."

"Can't right now, I'm on a mission," she says, waving and herding you into a deserted sitting room. "This is the back way to the ballroom. Come on, I'm really thirsty."

"Mind if I take my coat off first? God." You undo the buttons, ignoring her sulky look, and hold out your coat. "Where should I put this?"

"Here," she says, taking and slinging it across a chair. "Now come *on*. I just ate salted cashews and I'm so thirsty I'm spitting cotton."

"You know, bossy people don't last long in public school," you say, following her through a maze of rooms and finally to the juice bar.

"Not bossy, *assertive*." The sparkling starlight shot from the crystal chandeliers dances in her eyes. "And I know it's rude to correct a guest, but this is my house, Blair, not a public school, so . . ." She shrugs, your beheading complete, and turns her attention to the bartender, ordering a cranberry juice with three ice cubes and two stirrer straws.

You wait your turn to order, but it never comes. The bartender is hypnotized by the sight of Dellasandra's pursed lips sucking on the slim double straws.

"Yum," she says, dimpling up at him. "I love cranberry juice. Especially the color." She drains the glass and draws at the bottom until the ice cubes squeak in protest. "Another one, please."

You ask loudly for a Coke, but your request dies an unfulfilled death as Della leans forward, planting her elbows and resting her breasts on the bar while explaining the use of cranberry juice in preventing urinary tract infections to the mesmerized bartender.

And finally you realize that the monopoly is your punishment and you decide you don't need this. You can be ignored anywhere.

"Later," you say abruptly and take off through the crowd.

"Wow, you walk really fast," Della says, catching up and clinging to your side. "What's the matter, weren't you thirsty? Are you hungry? We have lots of food over there. Want some?"

"Not really," you say, refusing to look at her.

"Hey, stop." She halts your flight and waits until you meet her gaze. "I was being an attention hog, wasn't I? I'm sorry. My mother says I have to give other people a chance, too, but I *like* attention. My mother says if I don't mature and grow out of it, then I'll just have to become a movie star and spend my life posing for the paparazzi on the red carpet. Don't you think I'd make a great diva?" She laughs at your startled look and leans closer. "You know what? I'm glad you're pretty. I mean, I know it's not nice to say because people with pimples can't help it, but I think they're so gross. There was this homeschooled girl I used to play with sometimes, and she had the ugliest whiteheads all over her face. It was so hard to look at her. She was very self-conscious about them."

"Really," you say, at a loss and hating it. If Della were anyone else you'd ask if she was high or on meds or something, but the specter of your scowling mother makes you swallow the words.

"Uh-huh." She nods and her hair crawls across your arm. "My mom says nobody's perfect, though, not even me, and that compassion is a very important step in emotional maturity. Do you think that's true?"

"You're twelve," you say stupidly.

"Right," she says, as if your statement makes perfect sense. "My mother says I'm well-developed for my age but that I shouldn't let it go to my head because girls who get their periods early might also be at a higher risk for certain types of cancer." And then in the next breath, "Look over there. See how short that girl's hair is? I would never get my hair cut short. It's my crowning glory. My mother brushes it every night before I go to sleep. It is the *best* feeling. Does your mother do that for you, too?"

"What the hell was in that cranberry juice?" you mutter, and of course she hears you and lets out a gurgle of laughter.

"Sugar," she says, giggling. "I'm very susceptible. You're funny."

No you're not. She's just easy to entertain.

"Hey, that's a nice locket," she says, fishing it up off your collarbone and dropping it when you back away. "I have a gold one that was Jacqueline Kennedy Onassis's. My parents gave it to me for my tenth birthday. Do you know what they had inscribed on it? 'Our Pride and Joy.' Meaning me. They say I'm the best thing that ever happened to them. Isn't that nice? Is your locket inscribed? What does it say?"

"Nothing," you lie, and the afternoon stretches on.

Your mother is pleased with your good behavior and says so on the way home. She also confesses that if you hadn't been so amenable to the idea of reform, well, she and your father had considered either sending you to live with your grandmother or to a private boarding school.

There is no camaraderie in this shared secret. It's a barely veiled warning.

You don't care. All you want to do is get back to school and see Ardith.

But your mother comes downstairs the next morning and says she'll drive you in today. She's distant, distracted, and any ground you might have gained yesterday is lost because your hair isn't smoothed back into a ponytail and you're wearing too much mascara. She goes through your wrist bag, removes your makeup, and shakes the stray tobacco flakes from the bottom onto the counter.

"This is going to stop, too," she says, sweeping them into the garbage.

You're glad you had the foresight to wedge your cigarettes into your bra when you heard her coming. Glad you thought to wear the baggy red sweater she bought you for Christmas and that the black mesh T-shirt underneath it traps the pack and lighter in place. You have extra makeup in your locker at school, so you wedge your brush into your back pocket, smooth your hair into a ponytail, and conform without a peep.

Surface accommodations complete.

The traffic is bumper to bumper, the ride tense. You turn on the radio but she overrides your station with a Billy Joel CD. You toy with your seat belt latch and she lashes out, asking why you just can't sit still and behave for five minutes.

So you do. You turn your face to the window and sit stiller than death while humiliation seeps from your pores and anger rushes your exhales.

But nothing your mother has done so far is worse than sitting in the parking lot, watching Ardith get off the bus alone and stumble past you. Nothing is worse than knowing your mother is responsible for the pain in your best friend's eyes.

The bell finally rings. You go straight to homeroom and at the next bell you hook up with Ardith and relay the bad news. She's more numb than shocked.

Your history class is interrupted as Gary saunters into the room.

"Sorry I'm late," he says, sliding into his seat.

"Page one hundred and thirty-two," the teacher says irritably.

A moment later, as the teacher is droning on about filibusters, the whispering starts and a ripple runs through the room. You wait, anticipating the moment when the gossip surges your way, but instead of immersing you, it somehow divides and flows around you.

You poke the stocky kid in front of you. "Hey," you whisper, certain he's heard you because his ears are turning red and they always do that when you talk to him. "What's going on?"

Someone snickers.

The kid hunches over his desk, then leans back and stretches his arms behind his head.

You take the note and whisper, "Thanks."

Unfold the paper. Read it.

You & Ardith are gay. She just beat up
Marvin and got in trouble.

Your head jerks up. *"What?"*

"I said, 'I hope you're taking notes because you'll be tested on this,' " the teacher says. "Pay attention, please."

"Sorry," you mutter, suddenly aware of the class's voracious scrutiny.

So you play to the audience you refuse to look at, paste on a *lirgas* face, and roll your eyes like "whatever" while your mind scurries to connect the dots.

The gay thing is easy to track; big-mouth Gary and the night at the swim dance.

But Ardith's fighting with Marvin stumps you. What could he ever have said to make her disregard her carefully maintained boundaries and launch herself headfirst into the center of the adult universe?

It must have been bad, so you get a bathroom pass and track her down.

When you find her, she tells you everything and a dull pounding sets in behind your eyes because this is simply not acceptable.

It is *not* all right.

And while Ardith is hollow with fear, you discover you're anything but empty.

So you try to soothe her and spend a moment brushing out her cowlick. The gentle, rhythmic motions of brush-smooth, brush-smooth eases the despair in her eyes and reminds you of another friend you loved, and who fell victim to a malicious force.

And that's not all right, either.

The fullness inside of you demands satisfaction.

Kimmer needs to bleed. She needs to pay for hurting Ardith with some pain and humiliation of her own.

But she's powerful, popular and protected; there's no real way to get at her directly and come out of it without being punished . . .

Oh, yes there is.

"But what if—" Ardith says uneasily, watching your brisk preparations.

"Don't worry." If this works, if you really *are* the mountain and if Jeremy really can't resist the challenge, then you're home free. If not . . .

You sweep out of the bathroom. The fullness has infiltrated your mind and mapped out your victory. You don't question it. Whatever fuels you now will carry you through this and out the other side.

Your bathroom pass expired ten minutes ago so you buzz into the nurse's office for Midol and to cover your butt if the teacher asks where you've been. You scan the cafeteria, then plow on to the gym, your ugly sweater bumping the backs of your thighs with each stride.

Jeremy has an early lunch and usually spends it shooting baskets with his buddies. You danced with some of those idiots over Thanksgiving.

You pause outside the gym and hear the rhythmic *fwap! fwap!* of a bouncing basketball. Heart racing, you open the door and saunter in.

Six guys playing ball. Shirts and skins. Jeremy is a skins.

Nola, one of Kimmer's friends, is perched high on the bleachers near the front of the gym. She's bent over a book, so you disregard her for the moment. Smile to yourself as the players spot you and the game hiccups.

You wedge your hands behind your butt and lean back against the wall beneath the shirts' basket. Square your shoulders—posture counts—and watch as one of the shirts loses the ball to Jeremy.

He pivots and dribbles down the court. Sneakers slap and squeal against the glossy, wooden floor and the air grows turbulent as the players rush toward your basket.

Jeremy shoots. Scores.

"Nice job." You cock your head and your hair drifts across the side of your face. Your black bra shows through your sheer T-shirt. You scratch a lazy finger along your collarbone, just in case they haven't noticed yet, and the game stops as the six of them follow the languid movement. They're all so young. Were they, before Christmas? Were *you*? "You've got good hands. Want to teach me how to hold a ball?"

Two of the guys snicker and wipe their forearms across their sweaty faces.

The guy next to Jeremy elbows his ribs.

"Get offa me, butthead," Jeremy says, shoving him but still looking at you. His gaze is alive and curious. He's intrigued but not bedazzled.

You need more. You need to sweep him up in the all-consuming rush of the challenge. To make him an offer he can't refuse.

And it needs to happen fast.

"You want to know how to hold the ball," he says, slowly bouncing it.

"And maybe shoot a basket," you say, easing off the wall and ambling forward, closing the gap between you. "Score a few points. You know, just play the game." The clock is ticking. Nola will notice you any moment and yell to Jeremy, reminding him of his attachment to Kimmer. "You up to it?"

"Shit, man, he's up to it," the elbower exclaims as Jeremy stops bouncing the ball and watches you advance. "Basketball ain't nothing. He climbs friggin' *mountains.*"

"Oh yeah?" you say, holding Jeremy's gaze. There is only the two of you. Sweat beads his forehead. You reach out and wrap your hands around the ball, mildly amazed that you've gotten this far without losing him. You tug at the ball and he offers little resistance. You slide it loose and cradle it behind your back. "Must be the challenge, huh?"

He glances down and through your black mesh T-shirt. Settles on the valley in between your breasts.

You keep him with a deep breath. Your heart is pounding. Hurry. *Hurry.*

His Adam's apple bobs.

Yes. He's going to go for it. *With witnesses.* Anticipation ignites, sending waves of heat through your body. "I always win at keep away," you say and flash the ball out from behind your butt. "So come and get it, if you think you can."

He reaches around one side of you and you turn so that he misses. He tries again, and again you avoid losing the ball.

"Is that the best you can do?" Your teasing murmur is a siren's song, luring him onto the jagged rocks below the surface. You want this. You need this. You will have this.

"Get her, dude," the elbower says, voice cracking. "Get her."

"Get me," you urge.

His sneakers squeak and suddenly you're sandwiched between the wall and his hot, wiry body. His arms snake around behind you and his fingers tangle with yours, coaxing the basketball up until it wedges firmly into the tight space between the small of your back and the wall. He smells salty, like blood tastes.

"You can do better than that," you croon, pressing your lips to his ear. "Remember, you climb friggin' *mountains.*"

He locks onto your mouth. His teeth scrape yours.

Fuck you, you think deliriously, kissing him back. You widen your stance, arching into him and then receding, pulling him with you like an outgoing wave. *Fuck you all.*

"Hey!"

Nola has finally noticed you.

You curve and he instinctively follows, hip to hip, soft to hard, and you marvel at how easy it is to separate your mind from your body. Someday, when you run into Ardith's brother again, you're going to kick him in the balls and while he's writhing on the ground clutching his precious package, you're going to thank him for making your first time so bad that everyone after him can only be better.

Jeremy groans low in his throat.

"Mmm," you murmur in return, wondering how he cannot hear Nola clattering down the bleachers and across the gym toward you.

"Uh-oh," the elbower mutters. "Hey Jeremy, man, you're busted."

"Jeremy!" Nola yells. "JEREMY!"

Jeremy jerks loose, panting.

You straighten, letting the ball wedged behind you fall and roll off, and blot your damp chin with the back of your hand.

He blinks the glaze from his eyes, realizes, and backs away. Glances at the elbower, who gives him a silent, urgent eyeball message.

The front of his pants is tented.

The shirts and skins turn away, searching the glossy floor for their lost bravado.

"Two points," you say, smoothing your T-shirt. You glance at the sputtering Nola and want so bad to laugh.

"Oh my *God*," she says, gaping at him. Her hands flutter and grope for purchase. "I mean, Jeremy . . . oh my *God*, you are in *so* much trouble!" She wheels and races out.

"Thanks for the free shot," you say, and leave them all standing there. You put your sweater back on while you're jogging through the hall and trap your wild hair in your elastic band. You hum as you prance past the Guidance office window and when you catch Ardith's attention, you jerk your fist upright in triumph.

Her eyes widen.

You laugh, wave, and head for class.

The teacher is pissed.

You take him aside and, wearing your best repentant face, murmur that you had a problem in the bathroom and had to go to the nurse for um . . . stuff. You peek up at him from beneath your lashes, still shivering with the glory of the win, which he apparently takes for misery because he stops lecturing and tells you to sit down and try to catch up with the class.

You unleash your hair and bend low over your open book, shielded behind your curtain, and release a grin so wide it hurts your face.

You've done it. You've harnessed the nature of the beast.

Jeremy's cheating will sweep the halls in record time and this scandal will overshadow the other one because although the gay thing was intriguing, it was still about you and Ardith and you're not popular, which lessens the value of the gossip. Kimmer *is* popular, which automatically ups the ante. Her humiliation is priceless to everyone who's ever been ignored, dismissed, or razed by that crystal blue gaze.

What took you down has been used to raise you right back up again and you can't get in trouble for it. No one can tell on you, because making out with somebody else's boyfriend isn't against any school rule.

There's one more pound of flesh to exact, and although you'll go ahead and lay the groundwork, this one is ultimately up to Ardith. She's not going to like it, but she has to do it if she wants the gay rumor to die.

When the bell rings, you stream through the hallways, kicking up whirlwinds of whispers, delighting at the wide-eyed stares and the way the crowd parts to let you pass.

Gary's at his locker.

"Hey Gar," you say, stopping close to him. "Can I talk to you for a minute?"

He draws back in surprise, then his eyes narrow. "Why?"

You give him a speaking look.

"I guess," he says, shifting uncomfortably and studying the contents of his locker. "So what is it?"

You pick your next words with care, relying on your fledgling ability to predict behavior and use it to your advantage. "I just wanted to tell you that Ardith is really hurt by this stupid rumor. She was always on your side whenever we heard bad stuff about you and she never believed it or passed it on. She even stuck up for you back when Kimmer told everyone in the girls' locker room that you and Marvin must be butt buddies because neither one of you ever goes out with anyone. Girls, I mean."

"Get the hell out of here," Gary says, scowling. "I never heard anything about that."

"No kidding, because Ardith made Kimmer drop it," you say, and the sincerity in your voice almost has you believing the tale, too. "She said there was no way you were gay, and she said she knew it *for sure.* You know, the whole Burger King thing?"

"Yeah," he says, exhaling and running a hand through his stubbly brown hair. "I kind of figured she hated me after that."

You shake your head. "She defended you and that pissed Kimmer off, because you know nobody dares go against her. Now Kimmer's telling everybody Ardith's gay, which is like the dumbest thing ever, but it's really hurting her, Gary. You know why?"

"Why?" he says.

It's time. Guilt oozes from his pores.

"Because she's afraid you'll believe it, and then you'll never ask her out," you say, stifling a surge of triumph as his head snaps up.

"What? Bullshit," he says. "No way. Ardith hates my guts." But it's not so much a flat statement as it is a statement it sounds like he's hoping you'll deny.

"You see her with anybody else?" you say curtly.

"You," he says, and reddens. "Sorry. That's not what I meant."

"I know," you say, shrugging. "Look, you should just talk to her. Maybe something good will come out of it." You amble back a step. "Okay?"

"I guess." Preoccupied, he glances at the book he's holding, frowns, and chucks it into the locker.

"Well, I just wanted you to know what was up." You leave and can barely keep from jumping up and batting at the exit sign posted at the end of the hallway.

You breeze into Guidance, brandish your notebook, and call, "Homework assignment" to the guard-dog secretary in the main office, then head straight in to Ardith.

She's eating lunch alone in Mr. Everett's office.

You hunker down near her chair and share her food as you describe what's happened so far and what still needs to be done.

"No way," she says when you get to the Gary part. "I *hate* him."

"Well, he doesn't hate you, that's for sure," you say, studying a french fry. "Especially after I told him that you liked him."

"You *what*?" Her voice rises. "Blair—"

"Shhh!" You glance over your shoulder. "Come on, Ardith, it's the only way to end this. Get Gary on our side and he won't go blabbing anymore. Think about it."

"Oh God," she says, thunking her head down into her hands. "I don't want to go out with Gary. How come you get Jeremy, and I get *him*?"

"You could have had Jeremy, but you didn't want him," you say, miffed because she's missing the unparalleled beauty of your plan. "I can't do it all myself, Ardith. I'll look like some kind of nympho." You rein in your impatience. "Look, all you have to do is spend, like, a week dealing with Gary—"

"A *week*?" Ardith says, groaning.

"So you hold his hand in school for five lousy days and make him feel like king of the world before you dump him, so what?" you snap, leaving her the last fry on the plate. Jesus Christ, this is kid stuff. Why is she making such a big deal about it? "He went out of his way to ruin your reputation, remember?"

"I know," she says.

"So?" you say, watching her. "Come on, Ardith. I did the dirty work; all you have to do is sweep up. Do you want this rumor dead or what?"

"What about you?" She picks up the fry, examines, and eats it. "Kimmer's going to blame the whole Jeremy thing on you, you know."

"No kidding," you say, shifting and brushing a hand along the back of your pants, making sure your sweater is in place and you're flashing no crack. "Because if she blames him, then she'll have to admit that *he's* the one who betrayed her, not me. *He's* her boyfriend. *He's* the one who's supposed to be loyal. I have no allegiance to her life."

"I know," Ardith says, forking up a piece of her coconut custard pie and offering it to you. "But no matter what happens, they always blame the girl."

You open your mouth and the plastic tines slide across your pursed lips. "That pisses me off," you say, frowning and chewing. The custard is artificially sweet and the coconut ragged against your tongue. "I mean, he had as much free will as I did. He could've just walked away, but he chose not to. Why is that *my* fault?"

"Well, that's an easy one," Ardith says, lips twitching. "Because you're the friggin' *mountain*, remember?" she says, and then you're giggling, burrowing into her shoulder, and she's snorting laughter into your hair and when the secretary appears in the doorway, you wipe your teary eyes and leave without an argument because you've won this one and there's no taking that away from you.

You cruise into the girls' room.

Kimmer is there, red-eyed and huddled with Nola.

You smile. You can't help it. Lean into the mirror and brush your hair.

"Slut," Kimmer says.

You laugh because she's so predictable. You know you should ignore her but you're not willing to leave the spotlight just yet. "Tell it to your dog boyfriend. He was all over me, you know. *She* saw it. She knows. Hell, everybody knows." The fullness is back and the room is too small to hold you. "Sucks, huh?" You wedge your brush into your pocket. Your smile is dead. "So don't fuck with us again."

You walk out and pause in the hallway, adrenaline tremors rippling through your skin and out your fingertips. You can't remember when you've deliberately dashed so close to the edge and shouted a dare down into the void.

You touch the silver locket, nestled warm and safe beneath your sweater.

And smile.

Payback is fun.

Chapter 14

Ardith

So Blair pretty much squashed the gay rumor, but Kimmer didn't go down without a fight. She forgave Jeremy, of course, and leveled all her venom at Blair, guaranteeing her a front row-center seat in the Harlot Hall of Fame.

But Blair's new "slut" label came back to bite Kimmer in a way she hadn't anticipated.

You see, instead of humiliating Blair and sending her into the depths of loser anonymity, the spicy tag brought her notoriety and attention—*lots* of attention—from guys who apparently translated it differently than girls did.

I mean to girls, being called a slut is, what? The death of your credibility.

To guys, it's a major opportunity. A dream come true.

Especially to ninth grade boys, most of whom would sell their souls for a ten-second hand job. Let's face it: If you're an eighty-pound sapling with a squeaky voice, peach fuzz, terminal sweats, and sticky sheets and somebody drops a real-live slut into the mix, well, then hey, life is looking up and there's hope for you yet.

Watching them dog her bugged me, and knowing what they thought of her pissed me off, too. They didn't even know her as a person and yet they were so willing to believe the worst just because they hoped it would serve them.

And you know what else bugged me? How easily Jeremy betrayed Kimmer. I mean, I'd really thought he was different from the other guys. I thought he was decent, but then he went and got stupid, just like all the rest.

Blair said it was because she'd "harnessed the nature of the beast." I think it's even more basic than that.

Got breasts? Got power.

Think about it. No matter how guys bitch and moan about being used by girls or about girls who tease but won't put out, they're still the ones guilty of creating the power play. They enslave themselves with their own horniness and then, instead of keeping their vulnerability quiet so no one can capitalize on it, they advertise it! They up their own ante by *wanting* so much, and then price themselves right out of the market, because if they're telling us breasts are the gold at the end of the rainbow, then why should we just give them away for free?

I mean, where is it written that every guy who *wants*, gets? Come on. We're raised on Cinderella and they're raised on *Penthouse Forum*?

Talk about conflicting fairy tales.

Sorry. I didn't mean to go off on you like that. It's not your fault that Jeremy disappointed me, or that if you lumped all the guys I know together, they still wouldn't make up one whole, decent, trustworthy man.

Well, except for you.

You're welcome.

Yeah, I know there are a lot of different types out there. That's another reason I wanted to stay clean; so that when I finally met one of the good ones, I wouldn't have anything ugly in my past to be embarrassed about. Well, except for my family, but I figured I could always move away like my sister did and just pretend they didn't exist.

Now I can't even do that.

For a lot of reasons, but also because Blair's new slut label was rubbing off on me, too. In one morning I went from being a very private nobody, to gay, to a slut's best friend. And if I hadn't agreed to go out with Gary, I *still* would have been called a lezzie ho.

I hated it. All of it. The labeling, the attention, the games.

Blair laughed at me and reveled in her new notoriety.

"They're only sucking up to see what they can get off you," I told her during lunch, after Gary had gotten back in line to get me another order of fries and Blair's all-male fan club had momentarily abandoned her for their skateboards.

"I know, but so what?" she said, arching an amused eyebrow. "It doesn't mean they're going to get anything. It's not my fault they're determined to believe Kimmer's lies." She leaned back in her seat and stretched. "As far as I'm concerned we're all just buds, and sooner or later, when nothing happens, I figure they'll realize what she said isn't true."

"Then they'll dump you," I said, wondering when she'd gotten so much older than me.

She shrugged. "No great loss. They're only practice till we get to high school, anyway. I want to be ready for the real guys." She picked up her apple and sank her thumbnail into it, carving out the bruised spot and dropping it on our tray. "I don't really care who dumps me, as long as it isn't you." She examined the glossy skin, found it satisfactory, and bit off a chunk. Chewing, she said, "So your week with Gary's almost up. You ready to ditch him, or what?"

I met her probing gaze and looked away. "I don't know yet."

Gary returned and sat next to me. His sweatshirt smelled like wood smoke from his fireplace. He handed over my fries and two packets of ketchup. Bumped his knee against mine and, smiling, refused my money.

I caught our reflection in Blair's eyes.

And then she turned her head and we were gone.

This ice water's running right through me.

Keep talking. I'll be back.

Chapter 15

Blair

You know what's interesting?

Well, besides that full feeling I got from paying back Kimmer. It never actually left, you know; it just went dormant until I got mad again and then there it was, as big and powerful and fearless as it had been the first time.

What do I *really* think it was? I mean, is?

I think it's a gift. I do. Something good, coming out of something bad.

Maybe it sounds stupid, but I think it was there all along, only not totally formed yet, like an embryo sitting around gestating. Feeding on everything that happened, just like a fetus feeds off its mother. I think it was waiting to be born until I could handle it.

Because it's smart, you know? When something pisses me off and I'm all hot and raging, it's coolly and calmly calculating the most effective way to make my point. So I guess I have the best of both worlds now.

But that's not what I meant when I brought up something interesting.

What I meant was that for a while, Ardith actually thought I didn't mind the slut rep. Don't get me wrong, I *did* like the sudden attention, even if they were only ninth grade babies, but I definitely could have done without the slut thing. Nobody likes being called cheap and easy, especially when they're not.

But that was the chance I took when I got Kimmer, right? It was a calculated risk and it served its purpose, so I had to live with the fallout. The important thing was that it cleared Ardith's name and provided a spectacular distraction from that stupid rumor.

And, of course, that I couldn't get into any official trouble for it.

It's just weird that my bluff fooled Ardith, too. Normally she would have seen right through it, but this time . . .

I don't know, maybe she was so stressed that she wasn't really paying attention. Or maybe going out with Gary was getting to her, because it was definitely getting to me.

I never expected her to like him.

Chapter 16

Ardith's Story

Gary falls into step beside you after school. "Crazy day, huh?" he says, glancing down at you. "I hear you got suspended." His hands are wedged deep in his pockets and his tone is noncommittal, just in case Blair was wrong and you *don't* like him. You can tell his nonchalance is taking effort, though, because he keeps licking his lips. "That's beat."

"Yeah," you say, shifting the stack of books in your arms. Your teachers haven't been shy about providing you with tomorrow's homework assignments in advance.

"Here, give me some of those." Without waiting for your answer, he reaches over and appropriates most of the books. "Better?"

"Yeah, thanks." You don't look at him when you say it, but are surprised you let him take them. You're used to carrying your own load. You glance at his worn work boots and gauge his stride. He's slightly pigeon-toed.

"So you're gonna be out of school tomorrow, huh?" he says, shifting toward you as a jostling group of seventh graders surge past. They bump him instead of you and shrink away, calling, "Sorry!" Gary waves them off. "I mean, it's just a one-day suspension?"

"Yeah," you say and inadvertently brush against his arm. His altered position has thrown you off balance and invaded your personal space. You hug your notebook to your chest but the slim binder is sparse camouflage.

"That's gonna be weird. I mean, you *never* miss school." He blinks and looks away, his cheeks tinged pink.

The awkward silence stretches but doesn't break. Your jacket swishes as you walk beside him. You think of the times you've passed in the halls or caught him staring at you across the cafeteria and realize chance alone was not what sent him to the darkened football field on the night of the swim dance.

And you don't know what to do with this understanding, now that you have it.

The history classroom's door is closed. Gary catches hold of your arm and draws you into the alcove created by the break in the lockers. He scans your face. "So, uh, you want to go out, or what?"

Your back is to the cinder-block wall. Gary is between you and the hordes of students flowing toward the exits, and the armload of books are between you and him. The distance reassures you. "Okay," you say, surrendering.

His eyes are hazel brown.

You notice that as he's leaning in to seal your new partnership with a brief, surprisingly soft kiss.

"Cool," he says, straightening. He grins and slides an easy arm around your bulky, jacketed shoulders. "Come on, I'll walk you to your bus."

You go with him. The crowd parts and flows around you, but

gazes widen and the air stirs with whispers as this new development is noted and passed on.

You made a diorama once, back in fourth grade. Set a shoe box on its side, lid off, and painted dozens of blurred humans with black-hole eyes and circular, red mouths on the walls. Made cage bars out of wooden shish kebab skewers and set them halfway into the box, then glued the snarling, slinking, plastic tiger on the outside near the opening.

The art teacher gave you an A plus. Said the overwhelming humanity in the background made the lone tiger more vivid, made it stand apart from its surroundings, a stranger in a strange land, unable to effectively hide or blend, but protected from the gawkers by the same bars that imprisoned it.

She saw far more in that diorama than you did and now you wonder if it's become a self-fulfilling prophecy.

Awareness makes you unnatural. Your limbs are clumsy, your face hot and huge. Even your thoughts are disjointed. You know you should put your arm around Gary's waist but you're afraid he'll think you mean it. You can't just leave it dangling between you both, though. That's lame.

So you hook it around his lower back. Feel his muscles flexing beneath your moist palm. Beads of sweat crawl like spiders down your spine. You glance up and find him studying your face. He seems pleased.

You can't deal with this. There's nowhere safe to look. Are you smiling? You don't think so, and you should be. You have to, if you want this to work.

Do you want this to work? You hesitate, confused about what *it* is, and then remember why you're going out with him in the first place.

You try to match his loping gait as he slows for your shorter one and you both end up hopelessly out of step.

"Hey, we'll get it right," he says, grinning and squeezing you.

You look up again and he drops a quick kiss on your mouth.

People watch as you pass and you can't make them stop.

Three kisses from Gary.

How has this happened?

You walk into the teeming courtyard. Your bus isn't there yet.

The thin wind whips and whirls through knots of gathered students.

"You don't have to wait," you say, offering him a chance to leave. Chill air invades the back of your collar, freezing your seeping sweat and coating your feet in ice.

"No problem," he says, tucking you closer to his body. "I figured I'd take your bus with you and just head home from there." He smiles. "Okay?"

"Gary . . ." It's the first time you've said his name with no animosity attached and it sounds strange to your ears. "It's really cold and I'm gonna get in trouble because of the suspension when I get home . . ." Does he understand that he can't come home with you? That he can have no real access to your life? You feel a sudden surge of panic, and only the relentless gazes of the kids monitoring your progress as a couple keeps you wedged in the shelter of his arm.

Well, that and the fact that he's blocking most of the wind.

"Yeah, I figured," he says, nodding as your bus rumbles into the courtyard. "That's why I'm just going to leave you at the corner. I don't want to make it any harder on you."

"Oh." You don't understand this. Who is he, anyway? Not who you thought he was and his improvement is unsettling. Guys who yell, "Nice tits!" and tell people you're a gay whore don't see you home when there's nothing in it for them. Guys like that sit around your TV room every night, drinking and being gross. "Why are you being so nice to me?" you ask abruptly.

He draws back, startled. "What, you want me to be shitty or something?"

"Well, no, but . . ." Confusion knots your words, which might be a good thing as you weren't sure what you were going to say next anyway. "Forget it." You move out from under his arm and head for the bus. Glance back over your shoulder. "You coming?"

He doesn't move. "You still want me to?"

He's leaving it up to you and you wish he wouldn't. You wish he'd just bulldoze you along so you could sleepwalk through the week and, when it's over, wake up having invested nothing more than your physical presence.

You didn't want to have to think and you absolutely didn't want to see him as more than an asshole.

Gary's nose is red, but yours is running. You sniffle and wipe it on the back of your free hand. "Yeah."

His head dips once and he follows you on to the bus.

The driver quirks an eyebrow, forcing you to proclaim in front of the world, "It's okay. He's with me."

You find an empty double seat and slide into it. Gary drops in next to you. The heater has fogged the windows so you make a big deal of cleaning yours off, top and bottom.

The busywork ends when the bus lurches forward and you plop back into your seat. "I can take my books now," you say, glancing sideways at him.

"They're okay," he says comfortably, bumping his shoulder against yours.

And then he asks for your phone number and gives you his, too, even though you lie and say you won't be able to make any calls because of the suspension.

He nods like he understands and tells you how he got grounded over Thanksgiving for denting his father's girlfriend's car with his skateboard.

Somehow you find yourself laughing with him halfway through the story, but stop when you see the light in his eyes.

"What?" His breath carries the fading scent of Tic Tacs.

"Nothing," you say, and gaze out the window until your stop. You haven't laughed with anyone but Blair in ages.

When you rise to get off, you notice a fresh *Ardith & Gary* scrawled on the cover of your notebook, and the sight of it tilts something inside of you.

Grinning, Gary wedges the pen behind his ear and shepherds you down the aisle.

"Well," you say, as the bus lumbers out of sight. The sky is gray and the streetlights are already on. "My books?" You hold out your arms and he piles them full. "Thanks." Take a step backward. How is this supposed to end? And why isn't he saying anything? "Well . . ."

"So you're not gonna be in school tomorrow," he says, hunching his neck down into his jacket and shivering. The wind brings tears to his eyes.

"Nope," you say, teeth chattering. Your hands have lost all feeling.

"That's beat," he says, shifting from foot to foot. His gaze rests on you, flits away, returns. "I guess I'll see you the day after, then."

"I guess," you say.

He bites his lip. Looks around and edges you sideways, closer to the thick stand of pine trees at the edge of the wooded lot.

You sniffle. Sniffle again. Your nose *has* to stop running.

His face dips to yours. His lips are ChapStick soft and his skin ice cold. He pulls back an inch, then kisses you again. This one is slow and deep.

"I've been waiting a long time for that," he murmurs when it's over, resting his forehead against yours. "But it was worth it."

His features smudge and blur. He's too close to be seen clearly.

"You'd better go," he says, stepping back. "You're freezing." He smiles. "Maybe I'll give you a call tomorrow from school or something."

"Okay." You can't stop shivering. " 'Bye." You wheel around and take off.

It's the first time you can remember seeking safety at home.

You burst into the family room. The heat burns your bloodless hands and sends your sinuses into an immediate thaw.

Your brother, Phone Dent, and Broken Nose are sprawled on the couch, eating Doritos and watching a talk show episode entitled "Men Are Afraid of My Big Breasts."

"*Brrr*, shut that door," your mother calls from the kitchen. "I can feel the wind all the way in here."

You do, and head into the kitchen.

"Did the boys tell you the news?" your mother says, frowning down at the bowl of meat loaf mix. "Crap. I thought I had more bread crumbs." Straightening, she wipes a stray hair from her forehead with the back of her hand. Thick, pink half moons of ground beef are packed beneath her fingernails.

"No," you say, setting your books on the table and pouring a cup of coffee.

"Well, we had another exciting New Year's Eve," she says, turning back to the bowl of meat. She scoops out a handful and packs it into one of the three loaf pans sitting on the counter. "Your brother went out to get snacks for the party and the goddamn cops must have been waiting for him because they tried pulling him over again, and he just wasn't having any of it. They chased him for almost a half hour before they caught him this time." She stuffs the next loaf pan. "I swear, the cops in this town don't have anything better to do than stake out your brother."

"So he got arrested again," you say, wondering if it happened before or after you met Officer Dave on Main Street and whether he was involved.

"Of course," your mother says, snorting. "Nobody cuts him a break. Why should they, when they can get their jollies by harassing him?" She fills the last pan and opens the oven. "We had to go down and get him again and then go back out and get *more* snacks because they wouldn't let him take his stuff when they impounded the car. Can you believe that?"

"Wow." You gauge her preoccupation and decide to drop your own bomb. "By the way, I'm suspended tomorrow for hitting some kid in my class. It was no big deal, but we have a stupid zero-tolerance policy, so . . ."

"Right," your mother says, sighing and reaching for her cosmo. "First day back from Christmas vacation and zero-tolerance for a kid fight. The whole world's going to hell in a handbasket these days, huh, cookie?" She drains the glass. "I think I'll make mashed potatoes. Maybe they'll make your brother feel a little better."

You sneak an ashtray into your pile of books and head for your room.

Gary calls the next day during his lunch. He makes you laugh with another skateboarding story, then lowers his voice and tells you he misses you. You hang in the balance for a heartbeat, then say *me, too*. You feel like a heel when you hang up and get inexplicably angry at Blair for forcing you into this position. You know it doesn't make sense—Gary's the one who's hurt you, so you have every right to hurt him back—but somehow that knowledge keeps slipping away.

And somehow your week of using and dumping Gary stretches on to two, then four, then more. Blair isn't happy about it, but she has someone else now, too, a rich, spoiled new friend named Dellasandra that you have no say over, so you edit what you tell her in the few stolen moments you have alone together between classes and Gary, and reassure yourself that the growing distance between you is normal. She's never had a real boyfriend and doesn't understand the amount of time they take.

And during those frequent moments when you head in different directions and she walks to class alone, you remind yourself that if her mother hadn't banned your friendship this wouldn't be happening, anyway.

Despite all the time you're spending with Gary, you know you'll never risk bringing him into your house. If he doesn't get caught up in the partying, then being exposed to your mother's coy flirtations and your father's touchy-feely, good ol' boy act will alter his opinion of you. He'll expect things he isn't pushing for yet and if you ever break up, the class will know all the secrets you've tried so hard so keep private.

You watch him when he isn't looking and wonder what you have that keeps him around. Sometimes you resurrect the night of the swim club dance and imagine what his warm hand would feel like inside your cool, damp bathing suit top. If his hand would make you shiver like Blair's did, and if that one awkward, blurred exploration really *did* mean more than you're willing to admit, or if it was just something that happened.

You still don't know and sometimes that troubles you.

Gary calls one night during dinner and when you're done talking, you admit to your parents that you have a boyfriend.

"Well, isn't that sweet," your mother says, beaming. "You'll have to bring him around sometime so we can meet him, cookie. Bring his friends over, too."

"Fuck no," your brother says, scowling. "Who wants a bunch of rugrats crawling around here, getting in the way?"

"Stop it," your mother says. "Ardith'll be a sophomore this fall, it'll be her first year in high school, and of course she'll be bringing her new friends over to hang out."

Your appetite dies. You've suddenly become visible.

"Hey, that means new babes," Broken Nose says, waggling his eyebrows. "I say bring 'em on."

Everyone laughs and gets busy mapping out your high school years, suggesting ways to widen your circle of friends and advising you who to bring home.

"No coyote uglies," your brother says and then at your mother's curious look, "Means if I woke up with my arm around her, I'd chew it off just to get away without waking her up."

Your father snickers. "Ahh, the good old days."

"Well, I don't mind ugly, but don't make friends with anyone like that girl from Christmas," your mother says, scooping up a chunk of lasagna. "That kind will get you in trouble, cookie, and I mean it. Walking around like she's hot shit with her boobs stuck out to here . . ." She shakes her head, not noticing your brother's knowing smirk. "She'll get a bad reputation and that's one thing you don't need going into high school."

"*He's* got one," you say, jerking your chin in your brother's direction. "How come it's all right for him?"

"He's a guy," your father says, and shovels a forkful of food into his mouth.

"It's different for boys," your mother says.

"His rep ain't bad," Phone Dent says, reaching for the shaker of Parmesan. "He's a player. There's a difference."

"How convenient," you say dryly.

"Listen, don't get all freaked trying to figure it out," your brother says, leaning back and burping. "I'll find you some friends. The seniors always check out the fresh meat to see if there's anything worth going for anyway, and trust me, you need girls who can help you with makeup and clothes and stuff, because . . ." He gives you an amused once-over and shakes his head. "Christ, you look like a bag lady."

You stare at him, boggled.

"He's right, Ardith, we'll have to go shopping soon," your mother says, eyeing your droopy, black sweater. "You're not a kid anymore and you don't want everybody to think you're weird."

"Get some tube tops," Phone Dent says with a leer.

"Get bent," you snap and, ignoring the laughter, jam the final piece of lasagna into your mouth and leave the table.

Your room offers no solace. The locks that keep them out also keep you in.

You pace, and think of the grim reality of the next three years.

The sharp, hidden edges have finally been pulled into focus.

You need to see Blair.

It was weird.

I mean, I knew Blair had put herself out there for me and was taking a lot of grief, but there was something inside me that just kept whispering, *But you didn't ask her to do it. She did it all on her own.* Nice, huh?

It still shames me to think about how I just let myself drift away from her. I'm not making excuses, but going out with Gary did have a lot to do with it. He wasn't popular but he'd stayed back, so he was a lot bigger than the rest of the puny ninth grade boys and being his girlfriend protected me.

Not enough, though, because when life got ugly again, look who I ran to.

Of course I totally forgot that Gary was supposed to call me after supper, which kicked up some crap when I got home. I mean, I used to disappear to Blair's all the time and nobody ever even asked where I was going or noticed I was gone, but when my *boyfriend* called and all of a sudden nobody could find me, well, they couldn't have that, could they? God forbid I go anywhere without clearing it with my *boyfriend* first.

But that's another story.

The bad part is that for all the care I took not to bring Gary home with me, that one phone call changed everything between us anyway. Can't win, right?

Well, at least I got to see Blair.

But you know what? We weren't the same with each other. We were being forced into different worlds and no matter how hard we fought with what limited weapons we had, the time spent apart was doing exactly what her mother had known it would do.

What she had *intended* it to do.

Turn us into strangers. Give us more separate experiences than mutual ones.

I mean, I could listen to Blair's stories and she could listen to mine, but we weren't there for each other during the actual happenings, so these stories could never be *our* memories, like the swim dance or Christmas night. Our bond was stretching, instead of strengthening.

Maybe it's true that shared trauma brings people closer together—a common hardship, a battle to survive—because when times are quiet people relax and go their own separate ways. They're lulled into believing they've got everything under control and don't need what they did before.

Blair and I discovered we were at our best when life was at its worst.

You need to understand that, or you won't understand anything at all.

Chapter 17

Blair

Are you all right? You look a little funny.

Oh. Well, yeah, I guess being mad is better than being in pain. Are you sure you don't need a pill or something?

Okay, then.

We got lucky that night. My mother was at a fund-raiser making contacts, oozing confidence, and flinging down a gauntlet by saying how much she was looking forward to going up against Jeanne Kozlowski in court sometime soon, and perhaps the only reason they hadn't managed to yet was because maybe the assistant prosecutor was reluctant to break her winning streak . . . ?

I know. Nervy, huh? Oh, and you'll love this. You know what she asked before she left? About the race relations in my school and if there were any bias-type issues going on that the principal was trying to keep quiet. Any hot-button topics.

Yeah, I'm serious. And that's not all . . .

"Nothing? Well, I'm sure something noteworthy will come up," my mother said, shrugging. "People are incapable of maintaining civility for any length of time."

"It would have to be a case that you were absolutely sure you could win," I said. "You won't make judge by losing in front of the world."

She laughed. "Don't worry, Blair; from now on, any case I take will be a media magnet and a guaranteed ticket to the bench. I have very powerful backing these days."

So my mother went to her fund-raiser alone, leaving me with my father, who made a quick, furtive phone call and then sat around petulant and grumbling about not being able to go out and meet his, er, *colleague* for a drink.

God, you'd think an attorney would be able to come up with a better cover story.

So when Ardith called, all I did was ask my father if a girl from school could come by to help me with my homework. He jumped at it just like I thought he would and after I hung up with Ardith, he got back on the phone and whispered all over again. Five minutes later he announced that maybe he *would* run out, seeing as how I wasn't going to be home alone after all.

I know. His concern touched me, too.

So I told him I'd be fine and I really had to get this homework done so I could get a decent grade on it, blah, blah, blah.

Yeah, he believed it. He believed it because he wanted to.

Oh, come on. There isn't a kid in the world who hasn't learned how to get what they want by telling their parents what they want to hear, when they want to hear it. And if the kids tell you they're not doing it, they're lying because they know that's exactly what you want to hear, too.

What? What happened when Ardith came over?

Of course I was happy to see her. Why wouldn't I be?

Oh. Well, yeah, things had changed. I'd been seeing a lot more of Della than I had of Ardith. I mean, I had nothing but time on my hands and hanging out with Della was a way to fill it.

And yeah, okay, I was kind of hurt that Ardith had been blowing me off for Gary. I got the feeling that she was putting distance between us because I was supposedly a slut and, let's face it, the longer she stayed with him, the less the whole thing applied to her. And that was fine, except she left me out there all alone among the jackals, you know?

But I was still glad to see her. We'd been apart for way too long.

The problem was that it showed.

Chapter 18

Blair's Story

You can't stop talking, haven't stopped since Ardith came in because the thought of sitting with her in awkward silence looms like your worst nightmare.

"So it was really good to hear from you tonight," you say, padding into the kitchen and cracking open the window over the sink. Lift your hair off your neck and let the crisp, almost-spring breeze cool your skin. The sour scent of stress sweat has already overpowered your deodorant. "You want something to drink?"

"Okay," Ardith says from the doorway. "If it's not too much trouble." She picks at a hangnail.

"Not at all," you say, hastily dropping your arms. "I could make cappuccino." You fumble with the machine's porta-filter. "You still like it, right?"

"Mm-hmmm," she says. "Me and Gary go to the bookstore for it all the time. Do you ever go there? Gary says they make the best mochaccino."

"No, but me and Dellasandra have been to the coffeehouse up

on the highway," you say, measuring out the grounds. "The one where all the college kids go?"

" 'A Cuppa Joe,' " she says. "Gary said their prices are crazy. He said they charged, like, eight bucks for a mochaccino and it wasn't even that good."

"Oh," you say, watching the steam hiss from the espresso machine. "They do, I guess. I don't know. I don't usually pay." You get ready to froth the milk. You're rushing, but you need something to do. "So you and Gary are good?"

"Yeah, we're good," she says.

"Good," you say, nodding. The coffee gurgles and spits. You wish she would stop acting like a visitor. You wish you could stop acting like a host. "Do you want to sit in here or in the family room?"

"I don't care," she says, shrugging. "Wherever is fine." Pause. "What time is your mother due home?"

"Late, probably," you say, handing her a cup. "Why? Do you want to sit near an emergency exit, just in case?"

Her lips twist in a wry smile. "Do you blame me?"

"No," you say, and mean so much more. Does she hear how much you aren't saying? Can she still hear your thoughts? You don't think so, because the distance between you hasn't lessened any. "Let's sit in the family room. My mother'll come in through the garage and you can go out the sliding glass if you have to." You stop, recalling the last time Ardith used that door. Does she remember, too? You can't tell. Her face gives away nothing.

"So how *is* the infamous Della these days?" Ardith asks when you've chosen your seats in the family room. You've curled up at one end of the couch and she's taken the armchair near the patio door. "Still as obnoxious as ever?"

"She's getting better." Your voice is too high and bright and you force it down, trying to recapture the old, easy tone you took for granted a few months ago, but it remains out of reach. "I mean, she still says the most bizarre things and has to have everything *her* way, but—" You stop, feeling a spear of disloyalty. In the past you've parried every one of Ardith's Gary stories with a Della tale of your own and since it hasn't always been a picnic, you've confided that sometimes you feel like whacking her just to shut her up.

But now, when Ardith mocks Della without ever having met her, or without offering up a bad Gary story for you to mock in return, it just doesn't feel right.

Slowly, you lean over and set the cup down on the new glass table that's replaced the old marble one. You danced and bled on that rock-solid table, christened it with Red Deaths, used it for solitary dinners and loud, laughing meals for two.

It's gone now, junked by your mother.

And with quiet, unfolding horror, you realize that your history hasn't just been rewritten, it's been systematically and methodically annihilated.

You think of Wendy and the locket you've never taken off. Tug up your sleeve and trace the thin, white scar on your forearm.

Your history should count.

"If I tell you something, will you promise not to hate me?" you say, and although the words are familiar, the uncertainty in your voice isn't.

"You know I won't hate you," Ardith says, but her answer isn't as reassuring as it once was, because her tone leaves room for "unless you've turned into a total asshole."

Or maybe it's just your imagination.

You wish you knew for sure.

"Well?" she says, cradling her cup.

I'm afraid, you want to say. *I'm afraid I've lost you because I just realized that I've already lost me.*

Instead, you jump up and grab your jacket. "Let's go have a cigarette."

"Okay," she says and follows you through the sliding glass door.

"I'm usually out here alone," you say, lighting up and leaning back against the house. "Nobody knows I still smoke but you, so . . ."

"I've been alone a lot, too," she says, after a moment. "I mean, Gary's good and all, but it's not the same." Flicks her ashes. "He's not you, you know?"

"Yeah, I know," you say, even though you *don't* know because you've never had a steady boyfriend. You've never had anyone who could even begin to take Ardith's place. Well, except for Wendy, and confiding in the dead isn't very satisfying.

The wind rattles the tree branches and moans along the eaves.

You take a deep breath and tell her about Medford Jr., the son of a banker. Your mother introduced you at a hospital charity event and although she's never come right out and said so, you know your job is to please the sons of the powerful and the wealthy. So you give Medford Jr. an apologetic but satisfying hand job to make up for the fact—lie—that you have your period on his date night.

And he isn't the only one. There have been two others, both sporting casual, rumpled Tommy gear and frat boy manners, private school guys with waxed brows and trust fund egos who started out bored, cocky, and in the end whimpered like puppies at your touch.

The smell of them turns your stomach.

Your mother is pleased by your popularity but warns you not to tell Della, as Camella Luna knows her daughter isn't ready to date, and if Della knows you've had boyfriends then she'll want some, too.

Dating? Is that what you're doing while you're hunched up against the Porsche's passenger door with Ellsworth Collingswood III, or whoever the hell he is, drooling all over you? "Fine," you say, because you can't imagine explaining your life to Della the enchantress anyway.

You grind out your cigarette. Light a second one.

Ardith sighs and confides her family's plan for her future. How she's supposed to carry the torch and maintain the party house for the next three years so that her parents won't be forced to grow up and face their addictions.

"I mean, they don't get falling-down drunk every day, but Blair, they drink *every day*," she says, huddling deeper into her jacket. "They're alcoholics, but they won't talk about it. They get mad if you even try to bring it up." Her voice grows faint and you lean closer to catch her words. "What if they were different, sober? What if my father wasn't such a . . . *hound* all the time, or if my mother looked right *at* things instead of deliberately not seeing them, just to keep the peace? My brother probably would have been different, and I . . ." She kicks a stone and it bounds off the patio. "Maybe they think all girls padlock their doors and leave home the minute they turn legal. I don't know, you know?" She pushes back her hair. "But what if nothing bad ever would have happened if they hadn't always been drinking?"

You think of all she's told you, of the pinches and gropes performed under the guise of drunken teasing, and a chill skates down your spine.

Ardith's thinking, *What if they'd been better sober?*, and you're thinking, *My God, what if they'd been worse?*

She shivers when you say it, then stares unseeingly into the darkness and talks of Gary instead. Of going to his house after school when his father isn't home and making out on his bed, cradling his clothed, straining body between her thighs and absorbing his urgent, thumping rhythm until her muscles ache from the effort.

"He presses so hard that the seam of my pants almost cuts me in half," she says, exhaling a stream of smoke. "Does that ever happen to you?"

"No," you say shortly. "The guys I'm with don't linger at the bases, Ardith. All they want to do is slide straight into home, if you know what I mean."

"Oh." She stubs her cigarette out in the flower bed. "And do they?"

The wind is moaning again, echoing dully through the hollow spot inside your chest. It used to be Ardith who had all the darkest knowledge, but now you're the one with the hands-on experience. Four first dates, no seconds. All with skin contact, none with soul contact. No one wants you with your clothes on.

You crouch alongside her and, when your gazes are level again, say, "No. That only happened once."

"My brother," she says, and her face changes, opens into the Ardith you've needed and couldn't find.

"Yeah," you whisper, resting your head on her shoulder. Her down jacket sinks beneath you with a gentle, puffed sigh. "Everything's so messed up." You feel pieces of yourself crumbling and falling into the void. "It's like there's just nowhere to *be* anymore."

Ardith leans her head against yours.

Brittle leaves skitter and crackle across the patio, caught in the wind's ceaseless drive. They skate and skim, pirouetting, dipping, soaring, and slamming back down to the ground, only to be swept up again and carried along.

You're afraid and you say so. Afraid of sinking back into your black-hole life when she leaves and not being able to climb out of it alone.

"Shh," she murmurs, stroking your hair. "You're not alone. I'm here."

The night blurs, and for a piercing heartbeat you can feel the sun on your skin and the whisper of sleek, silky, golden fur beneath your hand.

Your best friend has just brought you home. You won't lose your way again.

Ardith leaves soon after that. You hug her good-bye and watch as she jogs away down the cul-de-sac, flashing in and out of shadows until she's gone.

Your father comes home, shrouded in perfume. "Did your mother call?" he says casually, hanging his overcoat in the closet.

"Nope," you say, closing your notebook. "You have plenty of time to shower." You meet his gaze and wave a hand in front of your nose. "J. Lo Glow."

He hesitates, wary, and searches your face.

You gaze back at him, composed.

"Good thinking," he says finally, flashing you a thumbs-up. "Oh, and um, I guess she doesn't really need to know—"

"No, of course not," you say, forcing a smile. "She'd only worry and what's the point? Everything's fine. We do okay together, right?"

"Exactly." The cold has tightened his skin and he looks suddenly young. "Guess I'll go shower, then." He heads for the stairs. "You should probably be getting ready for bed, too. It's late and there's school tomorrow."

"Gotcha," you say, returning the corny thumbs-up.

The house feels peaceful now or maybe it's you. You don't know and it doesn't matter. You and Ardith are together again and nothing can go wrong.

Chapter 19

Ardith

You know what killed me the most about what Blair told me?

That she was turning into the kind of girl my brother liked and my father liked to hear about. The kind that put out without expecting a movie first or a phone call afterward.

Well, not that my brother really *liked* them at all. They were just convenient whenever the horniness hit him, willing to give whatever he wanted and not showing hurt when he never even bothered to ask their names.

He never asked Blair's name, either, you know.

The hardest thing I ever did was keep my mouth shut when she was telling me about those rich guys. I wanted to grab her and slap that "who cares?" tone right out of her voice. I wanted to scream, "*I* care, you stupid thing! Why are you letting them use you like that?" But I didn't.

I just shut up and listened. Cursed her parents out in my head, of course, for not giving her a safe place to hide—

What?

Because you need steady ground where you *matter*, not where your father ditches you to go cheat with his girlfriend and your mother breaks you down and pimps you out to further her career—

No, I don't think I'm exaggerating.

I'm the only person in Blair's world who loves her as is, okay? Who wants to *hear* her and *know* her instead of just touch her or see what she can do for me.

And I was the only one forbidden to be near her. What kind of message do you think that sent?

Yeah, I'm mad. I'm mad for her and I'm mad for me.

Because we could have been anything, do you understand that?

We could have been something really special.

Chapter 20

Ardith's Story

You leave Blair's and you're the life of the ghost town, scattering the shadows and jogging down the deserted sidewalks, claiming them for your own.

Blair worried you at first. *You* worried you, because you wanted to run almost as soon as you stepped in the door. But you didn't. You stuck around, hoping her square edges would resurface from the smooth, round hole she'd been forced to fit into.

When they do resurface you discover they're sharper now, honed and jaded, and somehow *you've* become innocent in comparison.

The balance has shifted and for the first time you feel like the lucky one.

You pass the "No Outlet" sign and jog the rest of the way home. Slip in the back door.

"Ardith?" your mother calls from the TV room.

You shed your coat and hang it over a kitchen chair. "What?"

"Come in here."

The air is different. You go still, trying to separate the cold rush you've brought with you from the vaguely familiar but alien thread weaving through the lingering scent of tomato sauce and garlic, cigarettes and beer.

You recognize it and your legs turn to lead.

You smell Gary.

"Hi," you say, forcing yourself into the TV room doorway. The lights are dim and you finally spot him slumped in the corner of the couch next to Broken Nose. There are two beer cans on the coffee table close enough to be his and the fireball explosion on TV casts a momentary orange glow across his features. "What're you doing here?"

"What kind of a welcome is that, cookie?" your mother scolds from the love seat next to your father, frowning at you and smiling at Gary.

Gary glances up at you without expression. "I called but nobody knew where you were, so I was gonna go out looking for you, but your mom—"

"Connie," she says, waggling a playful finger at him.

"Connie said I'd be better off just coming over and waiting here for you." He shrugs, leans forward, and picks up a beer. Sips it. Glances at the movie. Settles back in his seat.

"Oh." You're the only person standing. You lean against the wall like a two-by-four propped there for later use and wait, face smoldering. Finally, you say, "Well, I'm here now . . ."

He glances up and you realize he's been waiting for your next push. He's been waiting so long that he has your whole punishment planned. "Movie's almost over," he says, draining his beer and cradling the can in his lap. He looks back at the screen, making certain you understand that Vin Diesel has become more important than you right now.

Your brother grins and shrugs. *Busted,* he mouths at you.

You stare at him simply because there's nowhere else to look.

"Come and watch it with us, cookie," your mother says softly, shifting and patting the spot between her and your father.

The sympathy, the knowing, the *welcome to the sisterhood* in her eyes is the only warm spot in the room so you dive into it, and as you wedge yourself in between your parents, sinking in supplication, a lackey awaiting the king's pleasure, your father drapes his arm around your shoulders and gives you a quick squeeze.

You close your eyes and start to die.

"Don't worry, baby, Gary'll get over it," your mother whispers. Her breath is hot and fruity. "You just let him throw his little tantrum, then look sorry and make nice. He thinks *he* won, you *know* you did, and everybody's happy again." She pats your arm. "Believe me, this is just the beginning. You'll learn."

A shudder rolls up and out of you, vibrating in waves across your skin.

"Cold?" your father asks without taking his gaze off the screen. He squeezes you again and the stale scent of old cigar smoke stings you into a panic.

"I have to go to the bathroom," you blurt and heave yourself away from all of them. Go straight into your room and wait. Pace. Will the movie never end? And then it occurs to you that it already could have and Gary might have just gotten up and gone home.

Someone knocks. "Ardith, Gary's leaving," your mother says. "Don't you want to come say good-bye?"

"Send him back here, okay?" There's nowhere else to do this without an audience and your punishment has already been public enough.

"Into your bedroom?" Her voice sinks in disapproval.

"I won't lock the door," you say, and the urge to laugh bubbles up into your throat, the urge to add, "Don't worry, if we decide to screw, we'll do it in the pool where everyone else does, okay?"

She leaves. Gary arrives.

You motion him in and close the door.

"Make it fast," he says coolly, shoving his hands in his pockets and leaning against your bureau. "I'm already past curfew."

Oh God, how you hate him for his studied indifference.

"Are you mad at me?" you say and hear the weakness in your voice. You face him, stand within touching reach, hoping he'll jump the widening crevasse and come back over to your side.

He shrugs. You haven't groveled yet and he won't sell his anger that cheaply.

"I didn't know you were coming over," you say.

He folds his arms across his chest. "So what, you just disappear and nobody knows where you are?" He looks at you. "Where were you?"

"I went to the mall." You don't know why you lie, but you can't take it back now. "I didn't think I was going to see you tonight and my mother was talking about going clothes shopping, so I figured I'd better see what was out there before she went on her own and bought me weird stuff." You touch his arm and gaze up into his face. "Don't be mad."

But he's not done yet. "Well, how did you think I'd feel, finding out my girlfriend's gone and nobody knows where the hell she is?" he says, unfolding his arms and forcing you to remove your hand. "And then I sit here like an asshole all night and find out that you weren't grounded after your suspension at all." His voice frays. "I mean, what the hell is *that* about? What're you, jerking me around or something?"

"No," you say. "No."

"I'm sitting there listening to everybody talking about all these parties that have happened, and the ones they're gonna be throwing, like your brother's big eighteenth birthday next month, and I'm thinking, shit, man, is that why you didn't want me over here? Because you got something else going on the side?"

"No," you say helplessly, fighting to keep your balance on the edge of the crevasse.

"Then what is it?" His face twists as misery cracks the stone mask. "I mean God, Ardith, what am I supposed to think?" He runs a hand through his hair and meets your gaze, silently asking if you're really what he needs you to be.

The part of you made to crawl is still cold with resentment, but its rumblings are stifled by the reward of Gary's mouth and arms, and forgiveness.

You don't question why you're supposedly in need of forgiveness, or why you're so grateful for receiving it. Your humiliation is tucked away beside your resentment because, as your mother said, you know you've won.

Only you don't dare look down to see which side of the crevasse you've chosen or whether you just stepped into the center and sank into the void.

Gary says good night to everyone and leaves.

You lock the bedroom door and close the lights.

Open the window and help him in over the sill.

You make nice the way millions have before you and you understand the sisterhood now, you understand that caring makes you vulnerable, it makes you give in and reach out, make excuses, go blind, struggle, wither, and bloom.

"I'm gonna get grounded, you know," Gary murmurs as he sits down on the bed and pulls you into his arms.

"You can go if you want," you say softly, so he won't think you're serious.

"Nah." He rubs his chin against your hair. "I think I'll stay."

"For how long?" you whisper.

He smiles. Kisses you and doesn't stop.

The room is dark but you don't need to see. His breathing drives you. You didn't know a sound could do that, didn't know a gasp or a low, wordless moan could make you want to cause another and another.

Your hands ease under his T-shirt before his are under yours. His heart pumps beneath your palm. You arch closer and he slides his hand up your stomach to your breast. Slips under your bra and yes, the feeling is as sweet as it was the night of the swim dance. Sweeter, with his face buried in your neck and his moist breath shuddering across your skin.

You kiss while you pry off your sneakers, while he peels away your shirt and bra, then his shirt, and gets tangled in the sheets trying to join you under the covers.

Naked from the waist up is dazzling.

Your bare feet mingle with his. His belt buckle brands your skin, his hand slips to your waistband and hesitates, as if expecting to be stopped.

You sigh. Permission granted.

Kissing, you both fumble with the belts, then the zippers. Trace the top of his briefs while he touches your panties, your joined breath like thunder in your ears. Stroke the thin, wiry trail of stomach hair below his belly button.

He presses your hand against his crotch, then does the same to you.

"Oh God," he groans softly into your mouth.

You can't answer him because he's crept under the elastic now, under the pale, violet-flowered nylon, and the gentle pressure of his palm is making you quiver. You slip your hand into his briefs and kiss him to keep his sounds from escaping.

Minutes later he goes rigid and your hand is flooded with warmth.

The pressure of his palm slackens and he rolls away onto his back.

"Holy shit," he whispers as you lean over the edge of the bed and fumble for something you can use to wipe off your hand. You find a T-shirt, swab each finger and give it to him. Lie back and listen as he blots and scrubs. Somehow it would be an invasion of privacy to watch him clean himself. Touching is allowed but looking is not.

"Thanks," he says awkwardly and the bed shifts. "Oops, missed a spot." He wipes the sheet. "Okay, all done." He stretches out beside you and nuzzles your neck. Kisses your cheek. Props his head up on his arm and smiles. "Hi."

"Hi," you say, looking back.

His palm settles over your bare breast like a bikini top. "You okay?"

"Mm-hmm." Your mind is teeming with questions you shouldn't ask.

"Did I do something wrong?" he says after a moment, withdrawing his hand. "I mean, if you didn't want to—"

"No, I'm all right." Are you? You don't know. "Why? Are you okay?"

"Hell yeah," he whispers, grinning and waggling his eyebrows. "What're you, kidding? Best night of my life."

You smile and try to remember who he's ever gone out with but come up blank. Are you his first girlfriend? You think so, but you won't ask. Your twin bed is too small for a threesome.

"So," he says casually. "Did you ever, like, go out with any older guys? Like your brother's friends?"

What is he wondering? Whether you've done this before with someone more experienced, or whether you'll do it again while he's not around? Or maybe he's thinking about how effortlessly he scaled your walls and breached your window. Maybe the route reeks of "enter" instead of "exit."

"No," you say, and your answer seems to please him because he cradles you close, with your head tucked into the curve between his neck and shoulder.

"Don't fall asleep," he whispers. "If *you* do, I will, too, and then we're really screwed."

"I won't." You couldn't if you wanted to. Your thigh is in the damp spot on the sheet and it reminds you of everything you haven't done yet. And then you wonder if you'll be obligated to go further and further each time now, if this one giant step is going to force an ongoing series of reluctant baby steps and the thought chips away at your contentment.

"Good, 'cause I love you, you know," he says and hugs you tight, squeezing your breath from your lungs. "I don't want to get you in trouble. I don't want anything to go wrong."

"I know, I love you, too," you mumble and pull away slightly.

Just enough to breathe.

Gary leaves within the hour, slipping back out the window as quietly as he's entered.

You stare at the wet spot on the sheet, then strip the bed and remake it. Scrub your thigh until it glows red. Put a towel over the new sheet before you lay down again, just in case something dangerous remains and seeps through. It's silly and you know better, but you're still not taking any chances.

You can't sleep. Your room feels different. Inhabited. Nothing has been moved, but everything is out of place.

You catch Blair the next morning and tell her you didn't come to her house last night, you went to the mall instead. And when you tell her why, she swears to uphold your cover story and quizzes you on the details of your encounter. You tell everything and are oddly pleased as she draws back and stares at you. It feels good to be the first to be loved.

"Oh my God, did you say it, too?" she says, clutching your arm.

"Yeah." Your cheeks are warm.

"You did? Really? Did you mean it?"

You can't stop your smile. "Yeah."

"Oh." She sits back, mulling it over. Frowns. "Even after he humiliated you in front of everyone? I mean, I know he was mad because you were gone and all, but still. And what about him drinking with your family? Weren't you afraid that would happen and that he'd turn scummy?"

You gaze at her, speechless.

"I just don't get it, that's all," she says doggedly. "I mean, you *like* him when he's nice, but you *love* him when he's mean? What's that all about?"

Your voice returns. You intend to tell her about the sisterhood, but something else comes out instead. "Why are you being like this?"

"Oh, like you wouldn't ask me the exact same questions," she says, snorting.

"Why are you trying to ruin it?" you persist because suddenly it seems very important to figure out which side of the crevasse you've chosen.

"I'm not," Blair says. "But God, Ardith, if he loves you so much, then why didn't he tell you *before* you got naked? And why did you do it anyway? I mean, since when do you reward guys for bad behavior?"

"He was upset," you say. "We were making up."

"You were groveling," Blair says, shaking her head.

The distance between you is once again increasing. Somehow you've ended up on the murky side, where high expectations sink like potholes and lame excuses swirl like fog. Is this the sisterhood your mother was talking about? Looking, but not seeing? Justifying, carefully picking your way through while hustling to make nice so you won't stumble and drop what little you have, regardless of its actual worth?

Or is Blair on the wrong side? She might be. She's never even had a second date, so how can she possibly know how it is between couples? Who is she to judge you?

The bell blasts a warning.

"You know what?" Blair says, gathering up her books. "I'm sorry. I don't know what my problem is." She forces a smile. "Maybe I'm just jealous."

"No, maybe you're just *right*," you say quietly, giving her a hip bump.

She laughs and bumps you back.

And now that you can see again, you notice all sorts of disturbing things. How when Gary meets you, Blair deliberately drifts away. How you let her go and turn to him without a moment's hesitation. You notice how close he keeps you in school and how he's started asking who's over your house when he calls at night. How his lean body folds to fit through your window and his growing familiarity enables him to race around your bases, barely touching down as he beelines for home.

His reverence of you has been replaced with self-assurance and casual possession. He's grown tired of your hand and keeps urging your head south. You resist and an uneasy stalemate reigns.

You've been together for almost five months.

Your parents invite him to your brother's eighteenth birthday bash and he lifts a beer to Broken Nose's drunken, "To legal age and sealed juvie records! Let's hear it for starting over and raising hell!"

You stand beneath Gary's arm, wondering how you became a part of this, watching as he downs four more beers and kids with the others. One of the junior girls spills a drink down her front and he calls for a wet T-shirt contest, which almost happens until your mother hears and promptly forbids a drenched carpet.

Your brother's giving out birthday kisses and a mock struggle breaks out as the girls hold him down for his birthday spanking.

Gary is stomping, clapping and shouting out each year with the rest of them.

Four. Five. Six.

You edge away. Skirt the crowd and slip into the shadowy living room. Stand at the window, shake a cigarette from your pack, and watch as the lighter flame shivers in your hand. Draw, exhale.

Nine. Ten. Eleven.

The porch light throws a golden blanket over the sprouting lawn. Spindly, yellow daffodils spear up in the empty flower beds.

You wish *you* were eighteen tonight.

Twelve. Thirteen. Fourteen.

Headlights arc onto your dead end and sweep away the shadows.

Fifteen. Sixteen. Seventeen.

The patrol car cruises slowly past, then brakes. The driver's window is down.

Eighteen. And one to grow on.

You come alive. Bolt past the back of the cheering crowd and out the door.

"Officer Dave!" You toss your cigarette, hurtle down the steps, and latch on to his door, laughing, singing. "Where have you been? What're you doing here? Oh my God, it's been so long!" You're not drunk so you can't tell him how much you've missed him, but oh, you have.

He tips back his baseball cap and his mustache curves in a smile. "How're you doing, Ardith?"

"Fine," you say and crouch so you're eye level. "How's your family?"

"Good," he says, gazing at the cars lining the street. "Party time again, huh?"

"My brother's eighteenth birthday," you say, making a face. "Why, did you get a complaint?"

"Not at all," he says, refocusing on you. "Just figured I'd cruise by. Funny that you spotted me."

"I'm so glad," you say, unsuccessfully stifling a shiver. The daffodils might be spring's but the breeze is still winter's, and you're only wearing a T-shirt and jeans.

"You're freezing," he says, shaking his head. "Where's your jacket?"

"I'm fine," you insist, scared he'll make you go back inside. "Really."

"Right." He isn't fooled. "Here." He reaches across the seat and hands you a whispery, blue windbreaker. "It's not much, but it's better than nothing." He watches as you put it on. "Add a couple of stakes and a few poles and you've got yourself a pup tent. Man, I think I'd better go on a diet."

"Stop. It's perfect," you say, giggling as the sleeves swallow your hands. "Well, I could always belt it." Funny how one thin sheet of nylon chases the chill from the night. You wrap the excess tight around you and lock your arms across your chest. "Blair's going to be so sorry she missed you."

"Yeah, so how's your sidekick doing anyway?" he asks, stretching. "I haven't seen her around lately, either. Her mother's building herself quite a reputation, though. She getting ready to run for mayor or something?"

"No, she—" you say.

"Hey!" The shout cracks the night. "What the hell is this?"

You spin around. Your brother is standing on the porch, Gary right behind him. The doorway fills with sullen partyers.

The sight slams you back into your skin and reminds you of where you are. Of *who* you are.

"Get in here, Ardith," your brother says, starting down the steps. "You don't have to talk to the fucking pigs. They've got no right to be here."

You look at Officer Dave in mute appeal, ashamed to even have to ask.

He holds your gaze for a moment and in that heartbeat between what is and what may be, you see what he sees; a skinny, needy kid wrapped in a too-big, borrowed jacket who, despite her intention to be more, is destined to be less.

"Ardith," your brother calls again. "Don't tell him jack shit. He can't—"

You raise a sharp hand without turning, telling him to stop. To shut up. Telling him, without words, how close you are to stepping back and letting him rant his way straight into jail. How small a sacrifice he would actually be.

"I'm sorry," you whisper to Officer Dave and the shivering starts as you shrug halfway out of the windbreaker.

"It's not your fault. Keep the jacket till I see you again," he says quietly, stopping you. His gaze flickers past you, holds and hardens. He shifts the patrol car into reverse, gives you a brief nod, and backs straight down the dead end past the rows of parked cars. His headlights sweep the wooded corner as he turns onto the main road and he's gone.

Your brother whoops and his friends slap you on the back for having driven away the fucking pig. Gary envelops you in a hug and gives you a sloppy, show-off kiss.

And then your father taps the second keg and the crowd flocks to greener pastures.

You slip into your room and take off the windbreaker. Fold it carefully. Rest your cheek on the slippery material for a moment and breathe in the sharp, cool scent. Place the jacket under your pillow next to your hammer.

Finish padlocking your door right as Gary comes lurching down the shadowed hall to find you. Beer makes him pushy and he backs you against the wall, nuzzling your neck and sliding his hands over your body.

"I want to be with you tonight," he murmurs, eyes snaked with red veins and lids drooped near to closing. He smells like family.

"Me, too," you say, and the pain in your chest makes you breathless. "But let's go back to the party first." And you kiss him good-bye and lead him back into the TV room, settle under his arm, and stay there as he drinks until he passes out, until the party-ers crawl away and you're the only one left standing.

You go into your room and padlock your door. Lock your window.

The next morning you leave while the house is still sleeping and meet Blair at the bookstore for coffee.

"I'm breaking up with Gary," you tell her, staring down into your cappuccino until your eyes stop burning and the ache eases enough for you to go on.

Chapter 21

Blair

I was glad Ardith broke up with Gary. I mean, I felt bad because she was hurt, but I'd be lying if I said I wasn't happy to see him go. He was taking up way too much of her time—

No, that's not selfish of me. Let me finish and I'll tell you why. Geez.

Although she'd quit doing that "go ahead, be a moron, I'll just endure all your embarrassing bullshit" thing with him, she was still altering herself to make nice, you know? I'm not saying Gary was a total jerk, because for a while he was better than I expected, but then he went and screwed it up anyway.

No, I didn't feel sorry for him. I mean, he was devastated—didn't even see it coming—but he brought it on himself. If he'd been paying attention to Ardith, *real* attention, the way he should have been doing if he loved her like he said he did, then how come he didn't notice the most obvious things about her?

Oh God, like the fact that she'd done everything she could to keep him out of the party zone for as long as possible. Or that she didn't drink or get high and that she'd never gone out with any of the jerks there who did. She didn't go all trashy like her mother or screw him on the first night they were together. She wouldn't even go down on him! Didn't he even *see* the limits she'd put on herself? Didn't he realize that Ardith was great because of *Ardith*, not because of her family or him?

She was the best thing in his life and he blew it, and hurt her in the process. And then he had the nerve to ask for a second chance.

No, he didn't deserve one. Because he willingly became an honorary asshole in her family's Partyer Hall of Fame, instead of being there for her.

Look, here's a clue. If you have a son, pass it on to him. When a girl says, "Pay attention to me," she probably doesn't mean, "Ogle me, have sex with me." She means, "*See* me. *Learn* me. Make the effort to *know* me. Pay attention!"

I'm sorry. I know. This freaks me out.

You're right. I do feel guilty for setting her up with Gary. I should have just done it myself. I mean, hey, I'm supposed to be a pro at putting out and getting out, right? Yeah, well, the problem was that he didn't like *me*, he liked *her*. She wasn't supposed to like him back, though, or get hurt again, dammit.

That's why I was so pissed at Gary, and at myself.

And especially at my mother, for making me sneak around to see my best friend, who needed more from me than just an hour over coffee. She needed a safe place to crash and because of my mother, I didn't have one to offer.

Because of my mother, I hadn't had one for Wendy, either.

I know. I'm shaking.

Because it all adds up, you know?

It all adds up.

Chapter 22

Ardith

Did Blair tell you that she didn't think Gary deserved a second chance?

Did she tell you that I gave him one?

Because I was lonely. God, that sounds pathetic, but it's true.

I mean, I still had Blair during the day, but she was Dellasandra's at night and on weekends so there wasn't much time left for us. And then school let out and it was summer, and you know what happens when my parents open the pool. I had to get out of there, only I didn't have anywhere to go or anyone left to go with, so when I ran into Gary one afternoon and saw that the distance between us wasn't as vast as it could have been, I said okay. Sure.

And you know what? It was hard.

He was different.

I'd hurt him and he wasn't gonna let it happen again, so the indifference that had surfaced when he was mad was there all the time now and he wouldn't let me get past it. His reactions were always distant and controlled, like he was holding himself out of reach.

He was different in other ways, too. He wanted more from me, faster. No dawdling around the bases, as Blair would say. His only goal was to slide into home.

No, I didn't let him. Maybe I should have, maybe things would have been different if I had. I don't know.

Weird, huh? I didn't have very much left to hold on to, but by God, I held on to my virginity. Like that was going to be my ticket out of here or something.

Anyway, what's left to tell isn't really about me and Gary.

It's about going back to the pine tree at the edge of the football field with my best friend and digging a hole. Dropping in two new hammers and an old screwdriver and then covering them up and walking away without looking back.

Chapter 23

Blair's Story

When you graduate from junior high your parents are in the audience, so there's no way you can run over and hug Ardith, which is the only thing in the world you want to do. But you don't because they're already pissed at you for neglecting to mention the big graduation dance and for not going because you supposedly didn't have a partner. The truth is that if you couldn't go with Ardith, you didn't want to go at all. So you didn't.

Ardith didn't go, either, because Gary wanted to hang out at her family's pool party and strip down instead of dress up. She said she stayed for ten minutes, then left him there and went into her room. It wasn't a good night.

Your parents take you to your grandparents' house the next morning so they can give you your graduation gift.

Your grandfather is a skin-and-bone remnant in an Adirondack chair placed in the sun. His eyes leak sadness behind his glasses and his fingernails are long, thick, and gnarled.

You bend and kiss his sunken cheek, shocked to be so much bigger than he is. He smells like Cheer laundry detergent and, beneath that, mushrooms. You remember when he used to smell like fresh garden tomatoes and how he used to pat your face with his gentle hand like you were something precious or easily bruised, like a big, red Beefsteak tomato ripening on the vine.

Your grandmother gives you a money card and a box of family heirlooms.

"The lace tablecloth is right on top," she says and hugs you like you won't see her again for a very long time. She gives you lemonade and angel food cake and turns away when your mother broaches the nursing home subject.

"Please," she says quietly. "Just this once, let's not argue."

Surprisingly, your mother agrees and goes on to regale her with her latest career developments and the fine, new young people you've been meeting.

You leave shortly after that because your parents are throwing you a graduation party that evening. You don't really care—no one from your school is invited, only your mother's associates and their kids—and so you sit as the hairdresser French braids your hair and the manicurist paints your nails a bland mauve. When you get home, you spell out LIRGAS with glittery alpha decals on every other pristine fingernail. Slip into the poufy, mauve dress your mother's picked out and paste on the mandatory mask.

You check your smile. Put some teeth into it. Your incisors seem pointier and you wonder if they really are or if it's just wishful thinking.

Before you leave for the banquet hall, your mother looks askance at your nails and says the silver locket doesn't match the rest of the outfit.

"Then I'll change the rest of the outfit," you say and flash your pointy teeth.

She walks away, shaking her head like you're hopeless.

This cheers you immensely and you go on to the party, greeting your guests and accepting your envelopes of cash with all the charm you can muster.

Della and her parents arrive late because she says they had to make a special trip all the way upstate to get your gift.

"Open it," she says excitedly, thrusting the bulky, rectangular package into your arms. She hops up and down, beaming, clapping, and nearly causing a busboy pileup. Her bra straps must be elasticized. "C'mon, Blair, I can't wait anymore!"

"Hold your horses, will you?" you say, laughing in spite of your irritation at being pushed. You're used to her bossy joie de vivre now and know how far you can go without forcing her hand. "I don't want to rush into anything here."

"Bla-*ir*, come on!" Della spins and tugs on your mother's arm. "Make her open it, Mrs. Brost! Please?"

"All right already," you say before your mother can order you to do it.

"Here, sit right here," Della says, pulling you backward into a chair and hovering above you like a brilliant, scarlet hummingbird. "Okay, now go ahead."

Her enthusiasm is drawing a crowd and you're definitely curious, so you locate a neatly taped seam on the side of the pink, foil-wrapped rectangle and rip it open to reveal an ornate, gilt frame.

"Oh, how pretty," you say.

"That's not it!" Della squeals, whipping her hair back over her shoulder. It splashes through your father's drink and he frowns, but doesn't comment. "Look at what it is!"

So you tear off the rest of the paper.

And it's a good thing you're sitting down.

"Read it," Della cries, prancing with glee.

But you have. And you can't. Your vision has gone black.

"Goodness, what is it, Blair?" your mother says, and the joviality in her voice doesn't quite hide the underlying thread of uneasiness. She leans close and her perfume roils around you in waves, cutting off your air.

"*I'll* read it," Della says, pulling the frame from your paralyzed fingers and holding it up. "It's a gift certificate to Golden Sunrise Kennel, good for one golden retriever puppy from the next litter out of champions Ladylee Linnea Sun and Masterful Boy's Precious Golden Doubloon, winners of last year's Best in Breed." Della bounces again. "Wait'll you see these dogs, Blair! They're beautiful and they're the best of the best. Ladylee's going to be bred again in July so her puppies should be ready for Christmas and my mother already said that we can all go up together and make a day of it!"

You hear her. You hear her mother say that normally they would have talked to your parents first but when your mother mentioned your old dog's passing, well, they just knew that a puppy would be the perfect gift.

Your tendons creak as you turn your head and gaze up into your mother's face. You watch. Wait. And when she smiles and says, "Of course, how wonderful," you look back down at your trembling hands with their fingers splayed out, palms flat on the table. And you stare at them until someone says, "Maybe she's in shock," and then you look up and smile at Dellasandra and her parents and everyone else. You smile and smile and when no one's looking, you turn the framed certificate upside down so you won't have to look at it again.

Because your mother's going to make you get that dog.

She's going to make you replace Wendy, just like she's replaced your home, your clothes, and your best friend.

You can see it all now and for the first time you realize that this temporary reform you've agreed to was never meant to end, not even after your mother makes judge. *Especially* not after that, because by then you will constantly be in the public eye and appearances will count even more.

This bubble you've agreed to climb into has sealed shut and will never pop open because it wasn't born of whimsy, soap, and water, but sculpted with intent as durable as glossy polymer varnish. And it hardened while you weren't looking, shrunk into a carapace, a seamless, custom-designed, full-body cast from which there is no escape.

Your mother will win her seat on the bench.

Your father will win his freedom.

And you will smile as you smother in your sheer, shiny coffin.

"I'm back," Della announces, as if you'd even realized she was gone, and plops into the seat next to you. "Here, I brought you a cranberry juice."

You hate cranberry juice, don't you? You thought you did, but now you don't know. The glass is cold and slippery with sweat. "Thanks." You drink it and still don't know if you hate it.

"I'm so excited," Della says and stops, gnawing on her bottom lip. Glances around and leans forward, curtaining off the crowd with her gleaming hair. "I'm not supposed to tell you this yet, but who cares. Guess where I'm going to high school in September?"

Her breath blows hot on your collarbone. "I don't know. Switzerland?"

"No," she cries, giggling and shoving you. "*Here*, Blair. With you, my best friend in the world! My mother's already talked to your mother and they both think it's a great idea because then you can be my guide dog." She laughs and leans against you, blanketing you in hair. "But not really a dog, of course. You can just show me around and teach me how to act, and we can join clubs and play sports—"

"But you're only twelve," you say.

"I know, but I'll be thirteen soon, plus I'm advanced study and my grades are spectacular," she says matter-of-factly. "My mother says I'll graduate with the highest honors and be class valedictorian, too." She sucks down the rest of her juice and bounces to her feet. "Want another one?"

"No," you say, staring at your empty glass. "I've had enough."

"Well, I'll bring you one anyway, just in case you change your mind," she says and heads off across the crowded room.

You can't do this. You won't.

You rise and beeline for the powder room.

Your mother is in there freshening her makeup. She stiffens when she sees you. Checks the row of stalls and finds them empty. Her expression is carefully neutral. "I imagine Della just told you the news."

"What are you doing to me?" you whisper.

"Oh Blair, please don't be dramatic," she says, rubbing the end of her eyebrow. She hasn't done that in a while. You must really be getting on her nerves. "What's done is done, and it can't be undone." She opens her purse and hands you a travel toothbrush and paste. "Here. You had onions on your vegetable burger."

You take them from her and face the mirror. Open your mouth and scrub away the offensive proof of your hunger.

"Believe me, Blair, I'm not entirely comfortable with this school arrangement, either, and if I could have found a graceful way to get out of it without alienating the Lunas, I certainly would have." She tugs up your neckline and frowns at your locket. "But I can't. Their support has been invaluable and we have to return the favor."

"I don't," you say and spit foam into the sink.

"Of course you do," your mother says, taking the toothbrush and handing you a wet paper towel. "Wipe your mouth. You'll have a wonderful time—"

"No," you say, blotting your lips, "I won't."

The temperature in the room plummets.

"Grandpa looked awful yesterday, didn't he?" she says, holding your gaze. "I'm sure your grandmother would love to have help with him this summer, and we could probably send your school records down, too. Just think of life then, Blair; housework, cooking, babysitting Grandpa while Grandma watches her soaps, going to the grocery store on the senior citizen bus. . . . It wouldn't be *my* choice, but if that's what you really want . . ."

The wail that rises inside of you never makes it out.

Your mother hands you a breath mint.

You take it, and the brief rebellion is over.

You meet Ardith the next morning at the bookstore for coffee. She asks about the party she wasn't invited to and you tell her everything.

"So what happens to *us* when Della comes to our school?" Ardith says, but she already knows. School is the only constant, available arena for your friendship and now that will be closed off, too.

You rummage through your pocket and hand her one of the two slim, silver rings you'd found in your grandmother's gift box of family heirlooms.

"Here. It says 'You and No Other' in French. I looked it up online. I have one, too." You show her your pinky and force a smile. "Happy graduation."

Ardith slips on the ring. "I don't have anything for you," she says quietly.

"You're wrong," you say. "You've always had everything for me."

The sun stays out for a little while, but then it's time to go home again, and this pattern continues all summer. You live and laugh with Ardith and struggle for every breath in the rest of your world.

You're Della's favorite person now and so you stay over her house occasionally, sleeping in a black T-shirt and boxers while Della wears Disney's Jasmine pajamas. You lay beneath the crisp, flowered sheets in the second twin canopy bed in the perky, pink room and watch as Camella Luna brushes Della's hair until it crackles. Listen as they discuss her mother's latest causes, her father's successful surgeries, and current events, like the effects of the monsoon season on low-lying Third World countries.

And when her mother tucks you both in and kisses you good night, you're so choked with jealousy that you can only whisper it back, while Della calls, "And don't let the bedbugs bite!" with all the blithe assurance of a child who's never been anything but the center of a benevolent universe.

"Floods are scary, don't you think?" Dellasandra says, rolling over to face you. The night-light shines on her and sinks you into shadows. "I would be so sad if a wave wrecked my house and I lost everything." She shivers. "Maybe we could start a relief effort in high school for the victims of monsoons, like they did with the tsunami or New Orleans. What do you think?"

You shrug. "Maybe."

"What's the worst thing that's ever happened to you?" she asks, her voice gossipy, with no trace of any past traumas. "Do you know what my worst thing is? My mother told me she was pregnant and I was going to have a brother or sister, but she miscarried in the third month and has never been able to get pregnant again. It's been four years. Isn't that sad? Of course they thought about in vitro fertilization and adoption, but in the end they decided that I was enough." She scratches her nose. "Sometimes it's lonely being an only, but not a lot. I'm not that good at sharing anyway. My mother says you'll help me with that, too, since we're both onlies and kind of like sisters now. So I guess my worst thing has a happy ending after all, huh?"

"I guess," you say, toying with your locket under the covers.

"Let's not talk about sad stuff anymore. Hey, I know! You should come to Hidden View with us," she says, sitting up straight. "It was featured in this book and you would really like it there. It's a bed-and-breakfast in the middle of the woods—"

"No thanks," you say. "I'm not into woods."

"But you'll love it," she says, throwing back the quilt and clambering out of bed. "I'm going to go tell my mother we have to take you there."

So the Lunas take you to Hidden View, a deadly dull historic house bordering a state park, where you sleepwalk while Della expounds on the characteristics of pinecones, fungus, and the waning of the moon.

And they take you down the shore, where Della overindulges and you wait outside a Seaside boardwalk bathroom stall while she barfs up cotton candy, funnel cakes, hot dogs, and half a pound of saltwater taffy. She covets the stuffed tiger you won and mopes till you hand it over, then gives it to a toddler crying in a stroller.

You feel like smacking her.

"Don't be mad," she says, prancing along beside you, oblivious to the stares. She's wearing red shorts and a tank top and looks like a flamenco dancer.

"I gave it to you because I thought you wanted it," you say.

She laughs. "I did, and then I didn't," she says, bumping against you. "Now neither of us has one, and we're equal."

And then she darts ahead to catch up with her parents and wheedles her father into dropping fifty dollars to win her a stuffed penguin, which she cradles in the crook of her arm all night long and never gives to any wailing toddler.

Her family carts you to an art museum. Della steers you into the Norman Rockwell room, where she squeals when she spots her favorite—*Girl at the Mirror*—and tells you her parents found an original sketch made in the course of developing the painting, had it framed, and gave it to her for her eighth birthday.

You feel like telling her you have Norman Rockwell's original head in a jar but you don't, because she'll probably want that, too.

Della's thirteenth birthday arrives, and besides receiving a bash that makes your graduation party look like a jaunt to Chuck E. Cheese's, she gets a diamond pendant and a four-day cruise to the Bahamas. While Della burbles and pores over the breathtaking travel brochure, Camella Luna takes you aside and explains that it wasn't Della who excluded you from this trip, but she and Dr. Luna.

And you listen, nodding like you understand while she tells you what an important milestone turning thirteen is, and how she and Dr. Luna wanted to make it a special rite of passage for Della, a family trip full of love and cherished memories of their daughter's transition from child to beautiful, young woman.

You smile, like yes, of course, that's wonderful, like you have so many cherished, family memories of your own that you would never think of denying Della hers.

Whatever.

August draws to a close. The Lunas return from the Bahamas, tanned and radiant. Della gives you a souvenir T-shirt and an earful about eating conch salad, swimming with dolphins, and the glory of being thirteen.

She also tells you that Ladylee Linnea and Masterful Boy are going to have puppies. You smile and say good. Spending the summer in a body cast has worn you down.

You've watched the Lunas watch their daughter, seen the soft, helpless pride in her father's eyes when he calls her an enchantress, and the constant affection between mother and daughter. Camella Luna braids Della's hair while waiting in line at the amusement park. Della tucks herself in between them after a nature walk. Dr. Luna brings home fresh bagels on "family Sundays," which is the only day you're excused from duty and are left to wander your own deserted house in something less than peace.

The summer is gone, used up, and nothing marks its passing.

You sunbathe topless in the backyard, half hoping Horace will show up to mow, but when his shadow blocks the sun and the gap in his shorts reveals his interest, you get angry, throw on your shirt and stalk into the empty, air-conditioned house.

You don't want Horace, and you don't want family Sundays, either. Or a stupid Jackie O locket or a white lace tablecloth or a designer wardrobe or a dog or another faceless date with sweaty hands and a raging hard-on.

You don't want anything you have.

You want to take Wendy for a walk and meet up with Ardith. Go to the raggedy little park in your old neighborhood and sit on top of the jungle gym with your bare feet dangling, trading secrets as Wendy snuffles the grass for hints of squirrel. You want to race Wendy into the kitchen of the old house, salivate at the scent of macaroni and cheese, laugh as your mother calls, "Shut the door! What do you live in, a barn?"

You want to be glad that her law practice is barely surviving because your father is still in the family and brings home just enough money to squeak by.

You were never an enchantress. Your parents never waited with bated breath for your next brilliant pronouncement or scoured the world for an artist sketch to make you happy, but for a while you were all together, four on a team, and you were pure.

But not anymore.

Life is fractured. You hate it. You hate your father for betraying your mother and your mother for betraying you. You hate Della for her stupid innocence and sheltered, easy life. Your classmates for their spiteful baby games and the rich boys who've showed you the types of games to follow. You hate Ardith's brother for crushing your ideals and the Lunas for nurturing Della's.

The scar on your forearm is thin and white, not big enough to adequately represent the blistering inside of you.

Your breath whistles in your nostrils.

You call Ardith, but she's out with Gary.

You don't know what to do. Your mind won't empty into the empty space around you.

If you could cry, you'd be howling.

So you remove the black-handled paring knife from the drawer. Slide the sharp edge across your forearm. The pain is relief, hot, immediate, and real.

Your blood is the color of cranberry juice, which you now know helps prevent urinary tract infections. You laugh at your thoughts as the blood snakes across your skin.

There's no vow to make this time, only temporary peace as the full blackness inside of you fades to a dull, numbing gray.

Your cell phone rings.

You start. Blink.

Blood spots the counter. You wipe it away. Blot your arm and pull the phone from your shirt pocket. Check the caller ID.

It's Ardith.

You answer it. "Hi."

"Blair?" Ardith's voice rattles. "My brother just got in a head-on collision and totaled his car. He was drunk and running and he wouldn't stop and he spun out and smashed into—"

"Is he alive?" you say, because you don't care about her brother but you *do* care about her, and her panic is scaring you. "Are you all right?"

"Yes. No. You don't understand," she says, and her terror is a hand clamped around your throat. "He hit Officer Dave." And she bursts into dry, racking sobs.

Your knees buckle.

Chapter 24

Ardith

God, I don't know if I can do this.

Tell you how Blair looked when she came over the windowsill into my room. She was . . . bloodless, except for the smear she left on the wall. Her skin was wax and she was covered in a clammy sweat. She said she ran all the way over, but I don't know how she made it on those wobbly, rubber legs.

Yeah, now I know it was shock, but I didn't realize that before. Maybe because I was in total shock myself.

I mean, one minute I was walking down Main Street, coming home from Gary's Labor Day picnic, and the next minute my parents screeched up, screaming for me to get into the car because my brother was in a bad accident and we needed to get to the hospital.

When we got there he was sitting on a bed in the ER with only a stitched eyebrow and some bruised ribs. There was a cop standing next to him acting pretty cold, though, and that's when I started to get a really bad feeling.

The first thing my brother said to my father was, "You'd better get me a fucking lawyer. They're charging me with attempted vehicular manslaughter."

"What?" my father said, turning on the cop. "What kind of bullshit is this? My son wouldn't try to kill anybody—"

"Your son is under arrest for the attempted murder of a police officer," the cop said icily. "And if Officer Finderne doesn't make it—"

I made a noise, a hoarse, wounded animal sound. "D . . . D . . . Dave F . . . F . . . Finderne?"

"Yeah, that's the dickhead who's been harassing me," my brother sneered, still brimming with beer muscles. "Like I was gonna pull over for him!"

But I was already out of the room, running toward the nurse's station.

Officer Finderne was in critical condition. He was in surgery.

Was I family? Miss, was I a member of Officer Finderne's family?

I wanted to be. I *wished* I was. I couldn't stop shaking.

The next thing I remember was being hustled out of the hospital by my parents, who had to get home fast and find my brother a good lawyer.

I ran in ahead of them and called Blair. I think she collapsed when I told her. I'm not sure. It's a little hazy. I heard her drop the phone and then all this weird scrabbling. I remember begging her to come over . . .

When I close my eyes, I can still see that blood smear on the wall.

School started three days later. Our sophomore year, the beginning of high school.

My brother was out on bail by then. He started his senior year.

You see, thanks to the overwhelming local news coverage of Assistant Prosecutor Jeanne Kozlowski, standing tall and grim at a press conference, vowing to prosecute this case personally, my brother *did* get a good criminal defense lawyer.

Chapter 25

Blair

You know that my mother decided to represent Ardith's brother.

No, she didn't know he was related to the forbidden loser Ardith, and Ardith's parents didn't know that their big-shot lawyer with the grandiose plan was the little slut from Christmas's mother.

All they knew was that Attorney Brost listened very carefully to what their son had to say about police harassment, leaned back, smiled, and said, "We're going to win this case. We'll use all the weapons at our disposal, including your spotless adult record and the media. I will expect you to go to school, go to work, go home, and stay out of trouble. If you follow my advice, you will not only walk away from this a free man, but the subsequent civil suit will make you a wealthy one. Appearances count. Do you understand what I'm telling you?"

And according to my mother, who burbled the story as I turned to stone in my chair, this handsome young man with the soulful, puppy brown eyes held her gaze and, without blinking, said, "Yes."

"This is it," she said, clasping her hands in front of her as if in prayer. "The one I've been waiting for. Of course if the cop dies it'll make things more complicated, but still, with the right jury, well, anything's possible. I'll have to make sure it includes a few angry, young males." She winked. "Little inside info for you, Blair. When you want to win, stack your deck and harness the nature of the beast."

I picked at the fresh Band-Aid on my forearm.

Humming, she opened the fridge and selected a Diet Pepsi. "Thank God his juvenile records are sealed and he hasn't gotten into any other trouble as an adult. It's imperative he stays spotless until the trial. I think I'll pull a few strings and get us a speedy court date, just in case. We don't want the media to lose interest."

Her confidence slapped me numb.

"We'll get all the right community backing, of course," she continued, her polished nail tapping like a metronome against the countertop, keeping count of her coup. "After our Christmas offering, the priest at St. Anthony's definitely owes me a favor. . . . Hmmm, I wonder if this kid was ever a Boy Scout? I'll have to check into that."

"I thought he was drunk," I said finally.

"Breathalyzer showed alcohol in his system but he wasn't over the legal limit," my mother said, waving a careless hand. "Youthful indiscretion. Boys will be boys. Or, on the other hand, he may have been drinking to avoid dealing with the trauma of being continually harassed by the police. Perhaps he was intimidated and didn't know how to handle it."

It was hard to think clearly over the sound of her purring.

"All it takes is a reasonable doubt and Kozlowski knows it. I'll guarantee you one thing, Blair. By the time this is over, that bitch will never forget my name again."

Horror was melting my mask. I rubbed my forehead and reshaped my features into bland interest.

"The harassment claim has potential, too. After all, this cop was so out to get him that he even circled the house on the night of my client's eighteenth birthday party, hoping to provoke an incident."

My mother sipped her soda. "There are additional issues to work out and Kozlowski's case to rip apart, but when I present my handsome, clean-cut, remorseful young client to the world . . ."

And then she kissed my cheek and zipped away to her office to plot her win, leaving me chained to the chair and screaming inside.

I know what you're wondering. Why didn't I tell her that her client was a dog and a scumbag . . . or at the very least, that he was the infamous Ardith's brother?

I don't know, maybe because it had been so long since I'd told her *anything* that I didn't know how to anymore. Maybe because even the smallest confession was too big and would have exposed too much. She would have had questions and if I had answered them, I would have lost Ardith forever.

Or maybe that's bullshit.

Maybe I didn't tell because I knew it wouldn't have made a difference.

Maybe I knew she wanted to burn Kozlowski more than she wanted to protect *me*. That the Christmas rape would have been *my* fault for letting him in, for not realizing that lust isn't love and groping isn't caring. Maybe I knew she'd be madder at my lying and deceit than at his brutal invasion. Or maybe she'd sell me out, tell me it didn't matter because he'd been a juvenile and he was an adult now, or that my story sounded weak because there was no evidence and I'd waited too long to come forward.

Maybe I knew all of that and just didn't want to deal with it.

So I swallowed it, listened and learned.

Ardith and I called the hospital every day. Resurrected prayers we hadn't said in years. Sent get well soon cards signed "your caring friends, your worried friends, your concerned friends Ardith and Blair," and even tried to donate blood, but we needed parental permission and that would have raised questions, so it was an automatic no-go.

I invaded my mother's files and made a copy of the hospital report.

We almost threw up reading it.

Broken jaw, split cheekbone, whiplash, punctured lung, ruptured spleen, bruised liver, and some kind of kidney disaster. There was more but I don't remember the medical terms.

And then the pictures . . .

I'll never forget Ardith's face when she saw what her brother had done, and what he was going to be found not guilty of. I thought she was going to go straight home and take a hammer to his head.

And I would have been right there beside her, with mine.

Because we knew that my mother would get him off.

And that when she did, it would be totally unacceptable.

Chapter 26

Ardith's Story

Time is not your friend. It doesn't care if you live fast or die slow, if you are or if you aren't. It was here before you arrived and it will go on after you leave. Time doesn't care who wins or who loses, if your life span is full or empty, honorable or shameful.

Time is indifferent. It simply doesn't give a shit.

You never knew it before, but you know it now.

You've battled long and hard to be better than you are, resisted the combined assault of nature and nurture, but you aren't winning anymore. You're not even holding your own. The Ardith you were hoping to be has taken to whispering an ominous *Fight fire with fire* in your ear, not seeming to care if her hands and her soul are dirtied in the process.

You hold her off. Bury her advice without examination because you're afraid of what you'll find if you look too closely.

You're afraid she'll make sense.

High school starts and so begins the blitzkrieg.

Gary breaks up with you in the hall outside your homeroom on the very first day. He doesn't look back when he walks away and later that afternoon you see him with his arm around a junior. They don't look awkward or new and you realize he must have been cheating with her all along.

Blair's mother gives her first round of interviews and your sober, earnest-looking, all-American brother stands quietly beside her. He's not allowed to speak to the media yet, but Blair's mother gives them a high-drama account of the pain he's suffered from being the target of the local law enforcement's ongoing reign of terror.

Yes, he's seeing a psychologist. Yes, he has a job. He works at the Gap after school and on weekends. Yes, he's trying to put his life back together.

The astounding part is that people seem to believe what they see. Maybe not everyone, like the girls he's screwed over or your neighbors or the rest of the police force, but they all operate under the radar anyway, especially the neighbors, who know that even if your brother does get convicted, the rest of your family will still be here among them every day and it's just easier not to get involved.

There are a lot of new people in town, though, thanks to the ever-multiplying McMansions and the easy city commute, and they don't know your family at all. What they see in the sound bite is a polite, good-looking, middle-class young man driven to extremes by the unrelenting vendetta of a strict-looking cop with a grudge, and then it's *click*, on to the Bloomberg channel or whatever, to check their stocks.

It's a farce, and it just keeps getting worse.

Your brother becomes some kind of cult hero, a representative of the downtrodden tormented by fascists, and supportive websites spring up everywhere. His Nissan is totaled but Mrs. Brost makes sure he retains his license, so he drives your mother's boat of a Cadillac to school. He never exceeds the speed limit and obeys all traffic signals.

Your parents begin to believe they are public representatives of the downtrodden, too, and in the interest of preserving the myth shoo everyone home. There are no more pool or keg parties, no skinny-dipping or girls to rub against in the shadowy back hallway. Your parents and brother still drink, of course, but only behind closed curtains, and not with anyone outside the family. Your father shaves his chin stubble and trades his faded T-shirts for new, navy blue cotton work shirts. For the first time in memory, your mother's Daisy Dukes go into hibernation before October and she puts on new Levi's. She dyes her hair chestnut brown and shuts down her adult website.

There is, after all, a civil suit to think about once your brother is found not guilty.

Reporters camp on your front curb, so you climb in and out of your window and cut through the woods to catch the school bus at a distant stop.

Your honors classes are no refuge as you share them with Della, who recognizes your last name from all the media coverage and takes an intense interest in you. She partners with you in biology lab and whispers incessantly about how you shouldn't worry about your poor brother because her best friend Blair's mother is the defense attorney on the case and everyone knows she's the best. And then she insists on introducing you to her friend Blair, and you become a threesome.

The situation would be laughable if it wasn't so grim.

The first week of school passes and you find yourself envying Della's incredible brainpower. Sitting next to her is like having a state-of-the-art search engine at your disposal. She knows things, lots of things, and as you try to absorb her smarts by osmosis, you wish desperately that *your* father was an acclaimed surgeon who shared all aspects of his work and education with you.

But he's not, and a bitter, resentful *It's not fair* rises in you whenever Della casually mentions her father's vast, in-home medical library or the surgery she's been allowed to watch along with a small and select group of med students.

It's just not fair.

You think of the doctors working to save Officer Dave and want to be one of them. You think of the photos you've seen and ache to slip into his hospital room and lay his borrowed windbreaker, which you still cherish, over his body in the hope of healing him.

It's a crazy thought, but you clutch at any straw because he can't die. If he does, there's no limit to what you might do.

Fight fire with fire haunts your dreams, wears down your will.

You confide as much to Blair, who doesn't disagree. Sleepless nights and trying days have left purple smudges under her eyes and a knife edge in her voice. She looks as frayed as you feel.

Something's got to give.

Your brother's first interview comes on the same day Officer Dave loses a kidney. You watch it on the news in the TV room with your family and study your brother's profile as he tips back a beer. You imagine rising and smashing the can in his smug face.

"Ooh, you look so handsome," your mother says, smiling at your brother and giving your father's drinking arm an enthusiastic shake. "Doesn't he look handsome, Gil?"

"Jesus, Connie, don't do that," your father says, wiping the spattered beer from his pants. "I was going to wear these again tomorrow."

"Hey, check it out," your brother says, leaning forward. "That reporter—Janica Silvain—had me stand on the school's front lawn so the camera guy could get the flag waving in the background. Mrs. Brost thought it was a good idea, too. She said it made a statement about liberty and justice, you know?"

"She's doing right by you," your mother says, nodding.

You watch as the reporter asks your brother what he'd like to do with his life once the case is over and he can put these dark days behind him. Your hands curl into fists as he gives her an angelic smile and says, "That's easy. I want to give something back to my community. Maybe work with little kids, give them self-esteem, and try to keep them out of trouble." He runs a hand through his hair. "But I'm also interested in, uh, medicine and I might like to study, uh, podiatry, too."

You stare across the room at him. He shoots you an enormous, shit-eating grin and puts his finger to his lips. There is, apparently, more.

"And I want to tell kids that if they need help, they should ask for it," he says in a nauseatingly earnest voice. "That's what all those professionals are for."

The reporter thanks him and closes the segment.

You sit like a stone as your parents say how good he did and watch as he drains a second beer. Listen as he mocks the reporter's willingness to believe him.

"Shit," he says, smirking. "When she asked me what I wanted to do with my life, what did she *think* I was gonna say? 'Rock 'n' roll all night and party every day'? I mean, come on." He folds his arms behind his head and grins at your father. "She was a real hottie, huh?"

"Who wouldn't be, with their own hair and makeup team?" your mother says.

The phone rings.

It's always for your brother these days, so he's the only one who goes for it.

"Well, I have to say I'm pleased," your mother says, swirling her cosmo. "I was a little iffy about remortgaging the house and betting the whole shooting match on a female lawyer, but now I have to admit that you were right, Gil. The ice queen does make an excellent attorney."

Your gorge rises like bitter gall. Are you and Blair the only ones in the universe who hope it isn't over yet?

"Uh, yeah, she is," you hear your brother say and he's looking at you.

It must be Blair, although she rarely calls. Worried, you start to get up.

"What? Yes, it is. Well, thanks." He shakes his head and waves you back down in your seat. "Oh, you did? Thanks, that's really nice." He leans against the wall and adjusts his crotch. "No, she hasn't. No, I . . ." He straightens. "Ohhhhh . . . okay, yeah, I know *exactly* who you are. Believe me, you're not easy to miss." His voice grows husky. "Mm-hmm. Oh yeah." He laughs.

You know that laugh. That tone.

"Give me the phone," you say, springing out of your chair.

Scowling, he straight-arms you. *Wait,* he mouths, annoyed.

"No," you say and dodge his arm.

"Look, it was good talking to you but I've got to go," he says hurriedly, grunting as he fails to fend you off. "Yeah, me, too. Looking forward to it." Frowning, he surrenders the receiver. *Asshole,* he mouths, shoving you as he passes, and plops back onto the couch.

Heart pounding, you take the phone around the corner into the living room. "Della?"

"Oh my God, Ardith, I can't believe I just got to talk to your brother!" she says, and her squealing bores a hole through your eardrum. "And he's just as nice as he is cute! I knew he would be!"

"How did you get my number?" you say, standing by the window in the darkness. If you accept eighteen spankings and one to grow on, will Officer Dave cruise up in his patrol car, smiling and ready to take back his windbreaker?

"Huh? Oh, Blair gave it to me," she says, and it sounds like she paces when she talks. "I called her because I watched the news and I wanted to tell you that my mother said it couldn't have gone any better, especially since the police department refuses to make any statements of their own, other than on that cop's condition, which she said makes them look like they're hiding something."

"It's probably just procedure," you say, pressing your forehead against the warm glass and searching the sky for the North Star. You need to make a wish. Badly.

"Oh, she knows that. She's a politician, remember?" Della giggles. "She just said that's what it looks like to the general public. Blair's mother knows it, too, and that's why she keeps publicly pushing the cops for more than they can give. She's hoping they'll say something that'll mess them up even more." Della laughs again. "She's *really* good, you know. I told Blair that, too. Her mother's *definitely* going to make judge."

So it's down to this. Blair knows what has to come next even better than you do, and since she gave Della your phone number, the decision has been made. All that's left is for you to do your part.

"I know," you say softly and close your eyes.

And as you stand there hollowed out, seeing nothing, wishing for everything, all the fragmented, unresolved pain that has been multiplying inside of you like virulent bacteria coalesces into something dark and unthinkable and, God forgive you, ultimately useful.

You push the thought away, violently, but it returns vivid and alluring, perfectly formed and easy to implement. Easier now than when you and Blair first discussed it, as the initial revulsion has worn off. It would solve everything, too, and leave you and Blair absolutely blameless. There's no way it can be tracked back or get either one of you in trouble.

Fight fire with fire.

Why not? The only punishment you receive will be from your own conscience.

Use her.

Your weakened resistance bucks once, then surrenders, exhausted.

Yes. All right.

You open your eyes.

"Public school is way more exciting than being homeschooled," Della burbles. "I mean, if I didn't go to school, then I wouldn't know you, and your brother would be just another news story, but now he's not. He's real, and I almost know him. And I was thinking . . . what if we threw him a support party? We could have it at my house, and take donations, and my mother could invite her richest friends—"

"I have to go now, Della." Your voice is calm and gives no warning as to what will follow. You recognize this and your new impassivity chills you.

"No, don't go," she says. "I want to talk about my idea. I wish you had your own phone. Then we could talk till bedtime." And in the next breath, "Listen, don't tell your brother about the party idea, okay? I want to surprise him."

Your heart gives one dull, hollow, speed-bump thud. "No problem."

"Good!" She sounds all smiles again. "Then I'll see you tomorrow. 'Bye. Oh, and say 'bye to your family for me, too, okay?"

"Of course." You hang up, wander back into the TV room, and sink into your chair. Begin a silent count and are only at four when your brother glances over at you.

"That girl you were just talking to," he says, stretching and propping his feet up on the coffee table. "She's a sophomore, right?"

"Yeah," you say, toying with the silver band encircling your ring finger. "Why?"

"The one with all the hair?" he says, tipping his head back into the cushions and watching you through sleepy, narrowed eyes.

"Yeah," you repeat, feigning suspicion. "Why?"

"Hey Gil, you gotta see this girl," he says, glancing over at your father and rolling his eyes. "Holy shit, and I mean it. She's got, like, long, black Lady Godiva hair and a pair of tits that just don't quit."

"Shut up," you say, as if you weren't counting on this. "There's more to her than that."

"You got that right," your brother says, grinning. "Bet it's hot 'n' nasty, too."

"Hair down to her ass, huh? They didn't make sophomores like that when I was in school," your father says, eyes gleaming.

"Hey," your mother says playfully, slapping his arm. "What am I, chopped liver?"

"Then? No," your father says. "Now . . . ?"

Hurt spoils your mother's smile.

"Hey," you say, and fling a pillow at your snickering brother. "You leave Dellasandra alone, do you hear me? She's never had a boyfriend and you are *not* gonna be her first." You wait, but he doesn't seem pissed at your bossing him yet, nowhere near as rabid as you'd expected, and for one sickening second you're afraid that maybe he *has* turned decent and your entire plan is doomed. Fear sparks and you push again. "I'm serious. She's a nice girl, totally innocent and way out of your league, so just leave her alone."

"Oh, and I'm not a nice guy?" your brother says, flexing his muscles. "Come on, I'm a stand-up dude. Ask anybody, they'll tell you. What's not to like?"

You snort. "How much time do you have?" Your disdain wipes the smirk from his face and, excited now, you shove a little harder. "Just stay away from her and I mean it. She's off-limits."

"I don't remember asking your permission," he says with a black look.

"I don't really care," you say, wondering if Blair has given Della a similar lecture on staying away from your brother yet and, if so, what her reaction was. You bet you know. "I'm telling you to stay away from her—"

"And I'm telling you to mind your own goddamn business," he says, scowling.

"Knock it off, both of you," your father says irritably. "We're all on the same side here, remember?"

You shake your head and push up out of your chair. "Forget it. I'm going to bed." You give them one last, lingering look—if this works, you will turn eighteen before you're all at home together again—and go to your room.

The hammer and screwdriver are still under your pillow. You pull them out. They seem melodramatic now, tools a scared kid would use to ward off boogeymen who lurk in hallways, testing doorknobs and seeking entry in the darkest hours of the night.

They served you well when your only weapons were physical and violent, protected you from the worst of it along with padlocks, minimizer bras, and lime green sweats, but you don't need them anymore. Not for this, or anything else. Those days are over.

You meet Blair back at the pine tree near the football field, hack a hole in the root-threaded dirt, and bury the old tools. Wipe your hands on your jeans and meet Blair's questioning gaze with a grim, confirming one of your own.

You've both outgrown the girls you were defending, and the ones that stand in their place are now armed with powerful, adult-sanctioned weapons.

Tomorrow.

The end will mark the beginning.

Chapter 27

Blair

Do you remember when I told you about my mother's melanoma and how its mutiny really freaked her out? You know why that was?

Because it turned deadly with no warning. No fanfare, no big announcement or parade, no shouted challenge. That cute, harmless little beauty mark at the edge of her eyebrow just sat there for years, all calm and passive-looking, being smothered with face makeup or bumped with hairbrushes or roasted in the summer sun, forced to soak up whatever my mother exposed it to.

And not surprisingly, it began to change.

On the outside, all was status quo—it kept its familiar, reassuring shape—but under the surface it was quietly mutating into something hostile, dark, and deadly.

Maybe the mutation was genetically preplanned and it had no other destiny from the beginning or maybe outside factors were responsible for its surprise shift to malignancy. Maybe both played a part. I don't know.

What I *do* know is that as soon as its outline blurred and grew, as soon as it bled one drop, hinting at its strengthening mutiny, my mother exercised her power promptly and efficiently and ridded herself of the troublemaker that had threatened her plans.

You know what that told me?

No hints allowed.

And you know what's funny? How all the lectures I'd gotten had slipped right past my defenses and soaked deep into my mind, whether I'd wanted them to or not.

How important my mother's own words would become.

"Sometimes we have to sacrifice one thing to gain something better."

"Appearances count."

"When you want to win, stack your deck and harness the nature of the beast."

So was I surprised when Della called and asked me for Ardith's number? No, not really. I would have been surprised if she *hadn't* called.

Why? Because after the first TV appearance she told me she thought Ardith's brother was really cute and asked if he had a girlfriend. She said it in a reverent, kid-with-a-crush-on-a-movie-star kind of way and in a sick, white-hot flash I knew exactly what had to be done.

So I told her no, I didn't think so, but I'd heard he'd had a lot of girlfriends, was way out of her league experience-wise, and if she knew what was good for her she'd stay as far away from him as possible. I gave her a serious lecture and actually forbade her to go near him. My mother would have been proud.

No, I did *not* tell her what he'd done to me. That's my own private business and besides, Dellasandra was definitely not ready to hear about something like that. I mean, come on, her favorite movie was Disney's *Aladdin,* for Christ's sake. How in the hell was I going to explain what happened to me to a girl who's never even been kissed?

And besides, the true goal wasn't to scare her away, but to lure her closer.

Did Della believe what I said about Ardith's brother being dangerous? No, of course not. I knew she wouldn't. I think she heard the "stay away from him" part and got her back up at being told what to do. Or maybe she decided *I* secretly liked him and was warning her off so I could have him all for myself.

But that's only speculation. She never came right out and said it, she just gave me one of those looks she uses for getting her own way, like that time at the boardwalk when she wanted my stuffed tiger and then changed the subject.

So I went along with her, but as an added nudge I let slip that Ardith and her former boyfriend, Gary, had just broken up. Della freaked when I admitted that yes, Ardith had been kissed, because that meant the three of us weren't equal anymore and if *I* somehow got myself kissed before *she* did . . .

Right. That would have been totally unacceptable. Della hates being last and absolutely will not be told that she can't have what she wants.

Sure, I knew that. I knew it the whole time I was telling her to stay away from Ardith's brother, too. I knew it *all*, Officer Dave. So did Ardith, when she was ordering her brother to leave Della alone. Don't you think she knew he wouldn't listen?

Do you finally understand what I'm saying here? *We knew.*

So after Ardith's brother did his first interview, Della called me for his phone number. She probably didn't think *I* had it—she was, after all, the sun that the rest of us mere planets revolved around—but she knew I could get it out of my mother's file.

And I did. My job was to accommodate Della, not deny her. My mother had been crystal clear on that point.

After I gave her the number, I had to sit there and listen as she burbled on about how handsome Ardith's brother was, and how it was a real shame he didn't have a girlfriend standing by him, lending support in his hour of need. I agreed with her, of course, and even managed to mourn his supposed loneliness.

In reality, Ardith's brother being lonely, horny, and impatient was *exactly* what I was counting on. Hell, if all went well, he'd end up in prison and never be lonely again.

But that wasn't gonna happen without a sacrifice, was it? My mother had called in favors and become a media darling—you couldn't turn on the local news without seeing her shining like Judge Justice on the courthouse steps, preaching the innocence of Ardith's sterling brother—and he, of course, had become the modern-day Beaver Cleaver, right down to the bashful toe stub and "aw shucks" smile.

Just another high-spirited boy next door, ma'am.

My house had a sick, rotten, Mardi Gras atmosphere going on 24/7. My mother hummed. My father sang. Lourdes tossed salads and Horace pruned all the tortured ornamentals in the yard, hacking off the tender, new growth and reinforcing the bushes' twisted, unnatural shapes.

Support for Ardith's brother flowed in and some idiot even started a fund to pay his legal bills.

No one in my world cared that you lost a kidney and got an infection that almost killed you, that your body was so battered that you could never be a cop again. No one gave a shit that you had two little kids and a wife who couldn't come out of the house without being bombarded by accusations of stalking and abuse of power, or that your reputation, once shredded, could never fully be repaired.

There was no room in this triumph for your tragedy, and that wasn't fair, so we changed it.

We mutinied quietly, using every lesson we'd been taught by every person who'd ever used us for their own benefit. We used what had brought us down to raise us up again. We shouldered and aimed our adult-sanctioned weapons of words and manipulation and self-serving drive, and when the scene was set, we settled in at a safe distance and watched the show.

So for all public intents and purposes, we didn't do anything at all.

All right, look. Think of us as a pair of those nature photographers who set out a sprinkling of corn in the winter, then hunker down behind a bush, watching as the hungry, bright-eyed little field mouse rushes forward to eat and is promptly seized in the jaws of a ravenous coyote.

Of *course* the photographers knew what was going to happen. They'd set the entire scene with absolute intent. And they *could* have stopped it. They *could* have stopped bystanding and run screaming into the middle and no blood would have been shed.

But if they'd stopped it, then there wouldn't have been an informative nature program, and those millions of interested viewers would never have seen the true nature of the beast.

No one blames the photographers for the mouse's untimely demise.

Because they didn't do anything. Nothing at all.

Chapter 28

Ardith

Blair is right.

On the surface we did everything we were supposed to do, as the friends and daughters of the families supporting my brother.

But underneath our compliant exteriors we were pulling strings and pressing buttons, fanning the fascination of the forbidden and maneuvering our predictable little puppets.

Yeah, we knew *exactly* what lessons Della needed to know to survive and we did not pass any of them on to her in time. Some were taboo because of her innocence, some we deliberately withheld because her innocence served us.

They were the same lessons we'd learned the hard way, too.

So are you still rooting for us, Officer Dave, or has the manifestation of our anger shifted us from sympathetic victims to heartless predators? Are you going to be one of those people who, no matter what happens, blames the girls?

Because my brother *could* have just given her a ride home. He had free will and made a conscious choice, just like Jeremy did, just like Gary did.

Just like we did, and you will, too.

You told us once not to be in such a hurry to grow up, but I don't see any way we could have avoided it. There was always someone out there ready to carve away another chunk of our innocence. I don't know why. Maybe because theirs was already gone and they couldn't stand the sight of our ignorant happiness.

That's what innocence is, you know. A blissful oblivion of what's coming, of what you'll lose and what you'll gain, and what kind of person you'll grow up to be.

I've been thinking a lot about what we did, or what we didn't do.

I brought your windbreaker back.

I don't deserve to keep it.

Chapter 29

Blair

So.

You know what's coming.

You've read the police report and seen the endless, frenzied news coverage.

There's more, though. The background stuff that nobody knows but us.

Wait. Let me light a cigarette.

Okay.

You meet Ardith in the far corner of the school's busy courtyard and assume your regular positions, backs against the brick wall and faces turned away from the morning sun. You can see everyone from here and everyone can see you, so you keep your conversation light and your intensity to a minimum.

You don't want to give yourselves away.

You've both dressed down, Ardith in a gray sweatshirt, jeans, and running shoes, you in combat gear, prepped for the battle of your life in a black turtleneck, jeans, and rugged-soled Doc Martens. The boots are new and your mother will undoubtedly seize them once she sees them, but by then, either way, it'll all be over and you won't need them anymore. They're only an outward declaration of a private war anyway, an unspoken fair warning to the world, and it will not be your fault that they didn't recognize it.

"You know why my brother traded his parking place up front for that one?" Ardith says, motioning with her chin toward spot number 132, only four spaces from the courtyard.

"Better to hang out?" you say, watching a bus rumble up and spew its student load into the courtyard. Not Della's. Not yet.

Ardith snorts. "Try better to watch girls in skirts go up the steps into the building."

"Nice," you say, and hope Della's wearing a mini today. You say as much and see Ardith's jaw tighten. "What?"

She shakes her head, avoiding your gaze. "There isn't any other way, is there?"

"Can you think of one?" you say, keeping your voice low despite the fierceness flooding your veins. "Can you think of *one other way* to end this, Ardith? Because if you can, now's the time to mention it." You wait, heart pounding.

"No," she says, glancing down at her silver ring.

"Right," you say.

It's going to work. You've thought the whole thing out, step by step.

You know that if you linger thirty seconds too long with Ardith and Della outside their biology class before the bell rings, Ardith's brother will saunter by on his way to business ed. In the past you've bailed early and left Ardith to hustle Della inside before this happens, but today . . . well, today you've worn the Doc Martens and they'll need relacing while the three of you loiter outside the classroom. You'll crouch, hair curtaining your face so you don't have to meet his mocking gaze, but Ardith will send her brother a snotty look and deliberately move in front of Della, as if to shield her from his substandard cooties. She may even mouth, *Leave her alone,* or *Don't even think about it* if he needs further antagonizing, if she can do it without Della noticing.

You know that sometime before lunch you'll head over to the payphone in the lobby and call in an anonymous tip to that reporter Janica Silvain's news hotline regarding Ardith's all-American brother and his new top-secret school romance. You'll tap out the number with a pen and hold the receiver with your sleeve. Your voice will be disguised, the cadence altered. Maybe you'll sound like a gay guy or an airheaded girl, maybe use an accent or a lisp. All you need is for the lobby to be empty.

At the same time, Ardith will be wandering the library, something she does often, but this time she'll be waiting for someone signed on to a computer to get up and leave for a moment. Once that happens she'll slip in, e-mail a similarly gossipy anonymous tip to the news station, and then go back to perusing the podiatry books.

You know that if you time it right, you can waltz Della past Ardith's brother at least twice more without changing hall routes to do it. You don't want to be obvious, though, so you may only do it once, near the end of the day, just to flaunt the forbidden.

You know the best view of the courtyard is from Ardith's history classroom upstairs and that at the end of first period her earring will fall off and be deliberately nudged under the back radiator, so it looks like it bounced there of its own accord. She'll worry aloud during lunch about having lost it, and after school, the two of you will have to rush up to find it, leaving Della waiting alone for her bus in the courtyard.

And you know that when school lets out, Ardith's brother always hangs by his car for a while, talking with friends and flirting with girls. When you and Ardith are there, you keep Della far away from him until her bus comes, but now that you won't be . . .

"Here comes her bus," Ardith says, glancing at you.

"Finally," you say, straightening and shaking back your hair. You touch your ring, then the locket holding the snip of Wendy's fur. Smile at Ardith and the promise of a bright future. You draw a great breath and, standing on tiptoe, wave at the virgin enchantress, who beams and waves back, always so happy to see you.

Honestly?

Della made it easy.

So did Ardith's brother.

Because they one hundred percent blew off all our warnings, Della with sparkly, badly disguised eagerness, Ardith's brother with cocky self-interest. They did everything exactly as we needed them to, and more.

Way more.

At some point during the day, Della, heady with the thrill of her own daring, caught up with Ardith's brother at the far end of the hallway, near the infamous blow job bathroom, and gave him a good luck card with a cute, cartoon puppy on the front. Inside, in her rounded, balloonish handwriting peppered with heart-dotted *i*'s and smiley faces, she'd written, *You will win this. Don't give up!*

Your friends know you're innocent! I can help you, so if you want to talk about my plan or about anything at ALL, just let me know. Your friend, Dellasandra Luna (the girl with the long black hair ☺). P.S. It was fun talking to you last night on the phone!

No, she didn't tell us she'd done it. The detectives found the card later on the Cadillac's floor along with her books, one of her shoes, her bra, and a fistful of hair. Ardith's brother had apparently panicked when Della did and had grabbed on to the handiest part of her, trying to finish the job before she got away.

He didn't, though, never even got her pants off, and I have to give her credit for that. She didn't make it easy for him and he's got the ruptured balls and loose teeth to prove it.

What? Oh, sorry. I guess I got a little ahead of myself.

Anyway, when the final bell rang, Ardith and I ran up to the history classroom and while she was crawling around, pretending to look for her earring, I was lounging by the windows, watching all the kids in the courtyard waiting for their buses.

Della came out first and stopped, searching for us. Ardith's brother followed maybe a minute later and immediately spotted Della standing by herself. He looked around, smiled to himself, and sauntered right over.

He said something and she lit up. He glanced around again and said something more. She shrugged and dimpled. He ambled backward toward his mother's car and she followed. He opened the passenger door for her and she slid right in.

"I can't find it," Ardith said, crawling along the radiator.

I watched, heart pounding, as Ardith's brother started the car and Della buckled her seat belt. Held my breath as they backed out of the parking spot and headed down the school's driveway. Released it as Janica Silvain's newsvan, which had been parked out on the street for hours, fell in line about a dozen cars behind them.

"Blair?" Ardith said, pausing.

I turned away from the window, looked at her dead-on, and said as calmly as I could, "Try over there in the corner."

She went still and gazed at me wide-eyed.

"Seriously," I said, caught up in an exultant, full-body tremble. "Look, I can see it from here." I wobbled past her, knelt, and retrieved it. Sat back on my heels and offered her the cheap, five-dollar hoop. "C'mon, we'd better go or we'll miss the bus."

"Really?" Ardith whispered without moving. "It's done?"

"Oh yeah," I said, rising and giving her a hand up.

That's all it took, you know. Her being in the car and him being horny as hell.

We still don't know what excuse he gave Della for taking the detour to his house, then pulling into the back woods instead of going down the dead end and into the driveway. Maybe he said he had to pick something up and wanted to avoid the reporters flocked on the front curb. I don't know. Whatever it was, she believed it.

God, why do we *do* that? Why do we always, *always* choose to believe?

Anyway, Janica Silvain must have thought she'd died and gone to heaven when she finally tracked down the Caddie and crept up on the scene, mike open and camera rolling.

And even though she told the cameraman to keep it rolling no matter what, at least she had the decency to drop the mike and call the cops.

At least that's the story she told when the local news station interrupted *Dr. Phil* and carried live coverage of Ardith's brother, bleeding, grubby, handcuffed, and with his shirt pulled over his head, being led into the police station.

Then they flashed to the reporter waiting outside the hospital in time to see a chalk-faced Camella Luna race into the emergency room.

The coverage skipped back to the police station when my mother arrived, reporters crowding her car and shouting questions as she bulldozed through them toward the door. The only time her stony demeanor cracked was when an angry-looking Janica Silvain yelled, "Your client was just arrested for attempting to rape a thirteen-year-old girl!"

"Allegedly," my mother said, pausing and rubbing her eyebrow.

"The video's been turned over to the police! Were you aware of your client's violent sexual nature?" the reporter demanded, fighting her way through the other media vultures and battering my mother's back with verbal blows. "Could this tragedy have been prevented? How will this affect his pending trial? The Lunas have already contacted AP Kozlowski and are vowing to prosecute to the fullest extent of the law! You and the Lunas were more than professional colleagues once, Mrs. Brost; do you have anything to say to them or will you continue to defend this *alleged* sexual predator?"

My mother didn't stop moving again and it was notable that there were no uniformed officers outside handling crowd control, clearing a path to her client.

I was sipping cappuccino and curled up in the corner of the couch when my mother finally got home.

"You heard?" she said, dropping her briefcase. It hit the polished marble floor with a thud and tipped over onto its bulging side. She didn't bother righting it, only stood there, hair messy, suit rumpled, and panty hose laced with runs.

"I heard," I said, watching her over the rim of the cup.

"It's all over," she said and went straight to her room.

So that's it.

Well, almost.

We're giving you these tapes, Officer Dave. You do whatever you need to do with them, okay? Erase them, turn them in, bury them in your backyard, whatever. We trust you to do right by us. We always have.

Oh no, don't do that. Come on now, stop. Please. If *you* cry, them *I'm* going to cry and I told you that I don't want to do that anymore. So you really have to stop now, okay? *Please?* You're getting your neck brace all soggy and spotting up your windbreaker.

Ardith? Oh God, not you, too. Go into the house and ask Mrs. Finderne to come out here. And bring some tissues, will you? Hurry!

Shhhh, it'll be all right, Officer Dave. It's a good thing. Really.

Because we cleared your reputation and we're not victims anymore. We did it, don't you see? We learned how to play hardball with the best of them and we won.

What do you mean, "Did we?"

leftovers

by laura wiess

Reading Group Guide

Reading Group Discussion

1. The Robert Frost poem in the epigraph states, "I hold it to be the inalienable right of anybody to go to hell in his own way." Do you think this quote is meant to apply to any particular character(s) in the story? What context for the novel as a whole does this quotation, as well as the Mother Teresa quotation, provide?

2. Discuss the narrative structure of *Leftovers*. Does the frame story make any part of the novel particularly compelling? Do you think that Ardith and Blair are reliable narrators? Why do you think the author chose to utilize this literary device?

3. At what point during the novel did you begin to realize that Ardith and Blair are disclosing their confession to Officer Dave?

4. Domestic dysfunction dominates the tone of this novel. How do Ardith and Blair each deal with the psychological abuse they endure in their homes? Are their survival tactics similar? How are they different? In what ways does each girl manifest the effects her family has on her?

5. When Blair's mother is anxious or unhappy, she rubs the scar above her eyebrow that is the result of a malignant mole. Besides the mole and the scar, what are some other symbols in *Leftovers* and what are their implications?

6. Blair states, "guys freak *out*" and "girls freak *in*" (p. 3). Where throughout the novel is her assessment of the differences be-

tween male and female behavior exemplified? Do you agree with Blair's opinion?

7. Were you surprised when Gary broke up with Ardith? How did the circumstances of their breakup relate to some of the novel's larger themes?

8. Blair states, "Ignorance of the outcome doesn't exempt you from the consequences" (p. 6). On the other hand, the concept of intent is especially significant in this novel. How does it apply to each character? Where throughout the novel are the consequences at odds with what was intended?

9. Ardith and Blair's relationship is maintained throughout the course of the novel, but in what ways does it transform? What effect do their peers at school, Ardith's brother, and Blair's mom have on their friendship? Do you think their friendship is one that is sustainable?

10. Ardith states, "Blair's mother caused some really bad heartache and while I'd like to say it's over now and I don't hold a grudge, I'd be lying" (p. 95). Do you think Blair's mother should in some way be blamed for the devastating attack on Dellasandra that Blair and Ardith carefully orchestrated?

11. The following lines provide the novel's conclusion: "[. . .] we're not victims anymore. We did it, don't you see? We learned how to play hardball with the best of them, and we won. What do you mean, 'Did we?'" (p. 232) Given the book's final sentence, what lesson is to be learned from this story? What do you think the future holds for Ardith and Blair?

12. Between Ardith and Blair, with whom did you most identify? Who do you believe is the better friend? Did you feel greater

compassion for either one of the girls or does either deserve more forgiveness?

13. Though their story is a predominantly tragic one, is there anything about Ardith's and Blair's school experiences that are at all reminiscent of your own middle school and high school memories?

14. Discuss the title. What is its significance?

Enhance Your Book Club

1. Before your book club meeting, take a stab at writing a short first chapter in the imaginary sequel to *Leftovers*. Where would we find Ardith and Blair five years in the future? Share your chapter with the group.

2. Read Laura Wiess's first novel, *Such a Pretty Girl*. In what ways does this novel differ from *Leftovers*? Has Wiess's literary style transformed at all between these two books?

3. Visit the author's website at http://laurawiess.com

4. For information about school bullying, visit the website of the National Youth Violence Prevention Resource Center at www.safeyouth.org, as well as www.stopbullyingnow.hrsa.gov, a site designed by and for kids and teens.

Author Questionnaire

1. *Leftovers* is your second novel. How, if at all, was your writing process different from when you wrote *Such a Pretty Girl*?

   Actually, my writing process was pretty much the same. A news story caught my attention, haunted me with compelling "What if . . . ?" questions, and characters were born to answer them. While *Such a Pretty Girl* and *Leftovers* unfold in different ways, with *Pretty Girl* happening in real time, *Leftovers* required both immediacy and distance. Plus, *Leftovers* has two main characters and covers a greater time period, so I was privy to a lot more of Ardith's and Blair's hopes, experiences, and family interactions.

2. How did you select the quotations for your epigraph? Did you intend to use them as part of the text before you wrote the book or did you find them after you had finished writing?

   Whenever I run across a quotation that appeals to me, I print it out and tack it up on a bulletin board. I was staring at the board one day during a *Leftovers* revision, skimming the same pieces of wisdom that I had so many times before but thinking about something else, when the Mother Teresa quote just . . . clicked. Right after that, while I was still excited over how perfectly it described Ardith's and Blair's hunger, I caught sight of the Robert Frost quote and thought, Yes, here it is: the beautiful, lethal, double-edged sword of free will.

3. Did you draw inspiration from any real-life events or acquaintances when you developed this story?

   One incident I drew from emotionally happened in my senior year of parochial high school. My friend and I had some free time in the afternoon, so we headed for the cafeteria. The radio was playing on the PA, and over in the corner a crowd of jock guys from assorted grade levels were standing in a closed circle, clapping, stomping, jeering, and yelling, "Go! Go! Go!" My friend and I were like, What the . . . ? and walked over to take a look.

   We peered through the crowd and saw another senior, a quiet, stocky kid who'd been tormented his entire high school career, trapped in the middle of that raucous circle. His school uniform was disheveled, his necktie knotted up around his forehead, and he was dancing frantically to the music, face beet-red, sweating bullets, desperate-eyed and unable to escape through the closed ranks.

Now, I was no angel and probably caused my share of heartache making it through, but when I saw this I freaked and without even thinking, elbowed through the crowd, grabbed this kid's arm, said, "Come on," and we plowed right out of there. I was so angry that I don't know what I would have done if the circle hadn't dissolved in grumbling and let us pass.

Which begs the question *why?* Why did they let him go *then,* when they wouldn't before?

Was it because someone had stood up for him, or because they were just looking for something to do, and figured they'd pass the time torturing him until it became inconvenient? Maybe they knew they could start back up on him later, when he was alone again, or maybe it was something as simple as deflating the mob mentality. Who knows? I still don't.

Anyhow, we went and sat in the courtyard, me furious, him humiliated and exhausted. We'd never spoken to each other before but that afternoon we hung out talking (and I'm pretty sure we each cut some classes to do it) about the different ways he'd been tormented, from the jock girls whining "Ewww!" and shrinking away whenever he walked by or changing their seats in class so they wouldn't have to sit next to him, to rougher locker room crap and just generalized cruel, constant mocking.

He was funny, kind, shy, lonely, smart, and interesting. Maybe a little scarred from a rocky home (and school) life. He was also visible but powerless, and his normal days at school were hell on earth.

We became friends for the rest of the year, stayed in sporadic touch for a long time afterward, and lost track of each other about seven years ago, when he and his family moved, and left no forwarding. I hope he's reaping the happiness in his adult life that was denied in his teen years because he didn't deserve that kind of treatment.

I also drew on knowing kids who came from party houses where almost any activity short of wrecking the place was fine, houses where the parents were hardly ever home, and from houses where at least one parent was always there to supervise. Kids who were encouraged to be whimsical, creative, adventurous, and kids who were constantly being groomed, molded, criticized, punished, and pushed to be *better, faster, more perfect, we have expectations and you must conform and fulfill them NOW*.

Intense stuff.

So, inspiration came from many places: stories, research, journals, news, memories, triumphs, tragedies, imagination . . . all combined, simmered, and fictionalized.

4. What inspired you to use two teenage girls as your main characters? Did you have to do any research to get inside the minds of Ardith and Blair? Would you like to focus on this particular demographic again in future novels?

The tragedy of school violence started me thinking about the possible difference in gender reactions to the daily, unrelenting stress and torment coming in from all sides, and wondering what would happen if it was girls instead of guys who were pushed to their limits. How much could they take, what would be the most damaging, how would they react, and what would happen when they reached critical mass?

I researched the effects of pressure on teenage girls, how it's internalized and may manifest later but bottom line, *Leftovers* is simply the personal, emotional evolution of two girls, not *all* girls, whose decision-making skills and reactions are fueled in part with kid-logic because they're too young to have the benefit of years of life experience to draw from.

I enjoy writing teens as main characters so yes, I very well may revisit this demographic. It all depends on the characters that show up, and the stories they have to tell.

5. Do you believe that America's teenagers, especially girls, are in crisis? What factors, particular to today's world, do you think contribute to their current condition?

   I tend to think more in individual terms rather than in categories, so while there are undoubtedly some girls in crisis, there are also ones that aren't. It also depends on the definition of crisis, and on individual perspective.

   Are Ardith and Blair in crisis? From an adult perspective, probably. From a peer perspective, one familiar with the normal day-to-day teen life, dealing with everything thrown at them, navigating the pressure to perform, temptations, little downtime, splintering families, the stress of trying to be what everyone wants you to be . . . I don't know. It can be overwhelming for adults, so why shouldn't it be twice as overwhelming for kids?

   So, *are* they in crisis, or are they simply products of the environments that we create?

6. What do you think can be done to combat domestic abuse and dysfunction?

   Please don't suffer in silence. Reach out for help. Get counseling, attend anger management classes, report the abuse, prosecute the offender, separate. Protect yourself and your kids, because what they experience growing up will, in some way, shape who they become and what they pass on.

7. Much of the action in the end of the story is in part the result of the manipulation of the law and the press. What are your thoughts regarding America's legal system and American media?

   When they both work they're hugely admirable; but when they go wrong, they are capable of doing great damage. Manipulating, and being manipulated by both, is nothing new; the key, I believe, is to recognize that there's always more to the story than meets the eye. I'm a big fan of pondering behind-the-scenes motivation and intent.

8. You focus on disturbing issues and many unhappy relationships in this novel. What effect did immersing yourself in these grim themes have on you while you wrote *Leftovers*?

I very much enjoy exploring all kinds of emotions, including the passionate but perhaps unhappy ones, so while I love these girls dearly, they also break my heart.

Ardith and Blair are very strong, loyal, committed, and in a lot of ways still naïve young girls who start out with the same hopes and dreams we all have—true love, fulfilling career, best friends, being heard, accepted and valued for who we are, a happy family, fitting in, etc.—and unfortunately learn some hard life lessons along the way.

The part that gets me the most is that everyone is so busy running their own agendas for reasons that make sense to *them*—killing a dog to preserve a carpet, enforcing a "No Violence" school rule without exception so other parents don't complain of favoritism and sue, forcing a kid to participate in a glossy, fake front for career advancement; or running a sleazy party house to feed a warped need—that they don't seem to realize that everything they say and do, or *don't* say and do, is impacting and shaping who Ardith and Blair become.

Given this, why would anyone be surprised when two young, impressionable girls, already on shaky family ground, grow desperate under what they perceive as an onslaught, absorb the lessons taught but interpret them differently, and then utilize what they've learned?

9. What lesson or feelings would you like readers to take away from this story?

   Actually, I'd like to consider this an invitation to readers to let me know what they end up taking away from this book. Do they feel for the girls, or do they blame them for not knowing better, even though these girls don't have a lifetime of adult decision-making experience to draw from? Do they see the hope in the story, and recognize that there *is* still time for them if only the right people pay attention, that they're capable of great love, caring and commitment, despite what they've been through? Will the girls use their free will to go on to live good, happy lives, or have their environments already doomed them?

10. What literary projects do you have planned for the future?

    I'm in the midst of writing and researching my next MTV book, so thanks for asking!